**"You rea[...]**
**do you,[...]**

"I'd say we don't like each other," she answered, keeping her tone just this side of impertinent.

"Would you now?" Iron fingers closed around her wrist as she turned away.

"It's true, isn't it?" Her hand was trembling in his grasp, her mouth unsteady as she tried to smile. "We haven't got along since the moment you first walked into the building, Nash."

"And to what would you attribute that?" he asked, a velvety menace in his deep voice.

"I...chemistry, I suppose," she said falteringly.

"Chemistry, yes..." He reached up slowly to touch her soft cheek with his fingers, his thumb caressing the sensitive satin of her full lower lip.

Christine shuddered helplessly. Oh, dear, she thought, what was this man doing to her?

**MADELEINE KER** is a self-described "compulsive writer." In fact, Madeleine has been known to deliver six romances in less than a year. She is married and lives in Spain.

## Books by Madeleine Ker

### HARLEQUIN PRESENTS

### HARLEQUIN ROMANCE

Don't miss any of our special offers. Write to us at the following address for information on our newest releases.

Harlequin Reader Service
901 Fuhrmann Blvd., P.O. Box 1397, Buffalo, NY  14240
Canadian address: P.O. Box 603,
Fort Erie, Ont.  L2A 5X3

# MADELEINE KER

## takeover

**Harlequin Books**

TORONTO • NEW YORK • LONDON
AMSTERDAM • PARIS • SYDNEY • HAMBURG
STOCKHOLM • ATHENS • TOKYO • MILAN

Harlequin Presents first edition April 1989
ISBN 0-373-11161-4

Original hardcover edition published in 1988
by Mills & Boon Limited

# CHAPTER ONE

IN ALL the six months since he'd taken over the *Herald*, Christine had never known Nash Canfield to open any conversation with social niceties.

'Do you know what goes on in Ransome Street?' he rasped as soon as she came into his office. 'Talk about a quiet country town—it's more like Sodom and Gomorrah.'

'Good morning,' she said calmly, knowing him too well to be rattled by this opening. The chaotic clatter of the newsroom faded behind her as she shut the door of his office.

She settled herself into the chair he waved her to, and crossed her slender legs.

'I take it you know what I'm talking about?' Nash demanded, drumming a devil's tattoo on the desk with impatient fingers.

'Yes,' Christine said steadily, 'I'm aware that the problem exists. As it exists in many towns of this size. I don't know the exact scale.'

'Nobody knows the exact scale,' Nash snorted, 'not even the police. But residents are very bitter in the areas affected, especially Ransome Street. Their lives are being made a misery.'

'Yes,' Chris nodded, 'I know that, too.'

'Yet as far as I know, this newspaper has never published an article about the situation.' He arched a dark eyebrow at her. 'Why is that?'

'Well,' she said awkwardly, 'traditionally——'

5

'Ah. That word again.'

He favoured her with a smile which added no gentleness to a face that looked as though it had been carved out of mahogany. In a good mood, it was more handsome than dangerous. In a bad mood, it was a lot more dangerous than handsome.

Nash Canfield had lived through a very rough childhood in London's East End. Everyone here knew that. He'd had to fight other slum-kids to keep the money he'd earned at his first job—as a newspaper boy for a big London daily. Later, he'd done odd jobs round the newspaper yard, making himself generally useful. His schooling had been negligible; he often said so himself. He'd learned almost everything he knew about the world from the pages of a newspaper.

At seventeen, he had been running errands between the newsroom and the Stock Exchange, and, at twenty, he had been contributing brilliant articles to the same paper's financial section. Stockmarket trends were his speciality.

He understood his topic so well that he'd built himself a massive fortune during his twenties, as he rose steadily upwards in financial journalism. Until he had had enough money to do what he'd dreamed of ever since he'd been a slum-kid, selling papers on a street corner: leave London for the provinces, and buy his own newspaper.

Those had been the origins of journalism's newest *enfant terrible*, the man who now owned the *Herald*. When you understood that, you realised that he'd always seen running a newspaper from the bottom up—not from the journalist's viewpoint, but as a business. As a huge machine for generating money, success, influence.

'Traditionally,' she said, 'the *Herald* doesn't have a record as an investigative newspaper.'

'You mean that our readers aren't interested in what happens on their own doorsteps?' he asked silkily.

'No,' she said patiently, 'I don't mean that. But I don't think people want to read about something as ugly as soliciting in their local paper.'

Contempt glittered in the dark gaze which jolted her from under lowered brows. 'You're the editor of the Wednesday Review. Doesn't this subject ever come up in all the copy that lands on your desk?'

'Well, yes,' she said. 'But——'

He tossed a file across the desk at her. 'There are half a dozen letters in there. All from women asking why no one's doing anything about what's happening to their area. One of the oldest and most respected parts of this town is turning into a red-light district. We owe them an investigation of why it's happening, and what's being done about it. And I think the Wednesday Review is the place to showcase it.'

Chris's heart sank about ten fathoms. Her Wednesday Review, a Canfield creation, was the *Herald*'s female-interest section. The family, the arts, fashion, health, fitness, women at work—things like that were the staple of the four-page, fold-out section that was almost a mini-newspaper in itself. She had often felt that it tended towards silliness, and it didn't always fulfil her ambitions to write seriously. But *this*——

'Are you sure?' she queried him, visualising a very large cat landing among her pigeons.

'You find it distasteful?'

'Yes, very!'

Nash drew a breath, black eyes glinting dangerously.

'This is *the* local paper, Yardley. Until we start reporting local news, good, bad or ugly, we don't have a
hope of competing with the nationals. Do I make myself
clear?'

She stretched her mouth in a thin smile. 'You make
yourself perfectly clear. As usual.'

The sarcasm bounced right off Nash's thick hide. He
leaned back, the silk shirt pulling tight over a faultlessly
muscled torso. Nash would have made a lethal boxer.
Or maybe a nightclub bouncer. He was six foot six, and
built to match, and that voice was grade three gravel. It
came from low, low down in his chest, and it could caress
in the most threatening way.

There was a sprinkling of silvery scars, too, not too
obvious against the tanned skin, but there all the same
once you knew where to look for them. The face of a
fighter. Not a brawler; a murderously controlled duellist
who'd long since learned to laugh in the face of life.

His idea of fun, apparently, lay in dangerously challenging sports like sky-diving, lone yachting, mountain-
climbing. Regular visits to the Mediterranean or
Caribbean kept that delicious tan fresh and deep.

'This has all the makings of a big story,' he mused,
obviously thinking fiercely. 'It has all the right ingredi-
ents—sex, human interest, shock-value. I want it on the
presses next Wednesday, before the *Chronicle* gets it.
We'll run a puff in the Tomorrow column on Tuesday,
and then again on the Inside column on the front page
on Wednesday.' With a hint of grim amusement, he
studied Chris's elegant beauty. 'Don't look so dis-
approving. God alone knows why you wear those glasses.
They make you look like a frozen schoolmistress.'

'They help me see clearly.' To tell the truth, she always
wore them when coming to see Nash. Partly as a kind

of flimsy defence, partly because she took a mean pleasure out of knowing they irritated him. 'Are you asking me to write the story?'

'I don't want you anywhere *near* Ransome Street,' he said sharply. 'I'm sending two men—Jennings and Tom Shoals. I'll be speaking to the commissioner of police myself. What I want *you* to do is tie in the story from the feminist angle. Speak to the local social workers, preferably women. Get a good, snappy, socio-political slant on the story. Oh, and find some good library pictures to go with it.'

Chris sat up very straight. 'I don't think this is going to work, Nash. When my father ran this paper——'

Nash's face hardened momentarily. 'Your father does *not* run this paper any more. I do. If you've got objections, then let's hear them.'

Chris shrugged awkwardly, not bothering to disguise her distaste. 'Why do you sound as though you need my permission at all?' she asked drily. 'As you've just pointed out, this is your newspaper now.'

'I'm more interested in your opinion than your permission,' he said in a velvety voice. 'So go on.'

'Very well.' She took a deep breath. 'Running an exposé of prostitution in this town will shock readers badly. It's hardly in the *Herald*'s best trad——' Warned by his arching eyebrow, she changed the word in midstream. '—interests. It might be expected of a London paper, but this is an old-fashioned, conservative district. Around here, it would be seen as an insult to the town's good name. Most people know that immorality goes on, but they prefer not to notice it.'

'Except the decent women who get accosted by complete strangers in Ransome Street,' he cut in drily. 'And who start panicking if their teenage daughters are ten minutes late getting home.'

'All right.' She conceded the point tiredly. He would never understand. He was a big-city man. He hadn't been born in this town, hadn't lived in it all his life, the way she had done. 'But it will also be seen as deliberate, salacious, muck-raking. It will alienate as many readers as it attracts. Worse,' she pursued her point, 'the sort of readers it's likely to attract are just temporary ones. The people it'll alienate are the backbone of our readership.'

'Like Colonel Blimp,' Nash suggested drily, referring to a retired Army officer who was a regular complainer in the *Herald*'s letter page.

'Colonel Ball has had a subscription to the *Herald* all his life,' she pointed out. 'He was a close friend of my father——'

'Look,' he said, leaning forward, 'it's up to you to see that the story comes across as serious, and not frivolous. That's part of your job. But the whole affair reeks of news-value—and news-value is what running a newspaper is all about.'

'Is that another word for publicity?' she asked sweetly.

'Don't knock it! This single story could double our circulation by next weekend. And some of those new readers might just stay. The *Herald* is never going to make a profit until it's been dragged—kicking and screaming, if necessary—into the twentieth century. How long are we going to keep pretending that nothing nasty ever happens here?'

'I know, but——'

'I knew you'd understand. We'll talk about it at an ECC meeting if you really have doubts. We can go through all the pros and cons there.'

Chris sighed inwardly. The editorial consultative committee meetings were something of a joke, anyway. And when Nash had the bit between his teeth, no one was likely to stop him . . .

Why, she wondered for the hundredth time that year, did he insist on discussing so much of the *Herald*'s business with her? Once, she'd had the idea that he respected her opinions. Chris was, after all, Sam Yardley's only daughter, and the person who probably knew the paper's history best.

But she'd long since given up the notion that he really valued her advice. Nash did whatever he planned anyway, regardless of her approval or disapproval. No, there was another, far more subtle reason. He used her, and her very close association with this newspaper, to give some kind of legitimacy to his own radical designs for it. Because she'd been the *Lancashire Herald*'s mascot ever since babyhood, and, though she'd never been their leader the way Dad had been, she would always be the pet of everyone in the building . . .

Without warning, his scowl eased, and he shifted from threat into charm. 'Listen, Chris,' he went on in an intimate, velvety purr which had an odd effect on the marrow in her bones, 'I've got a peach of an assignment for you in the mean time. Something short, sweet, and glamorous.'

'Yes?' she said cautiously.

'I've just been informed that Duncan Anderson is renting a farmhouse out above the gorge.' He glanced at her to see her reaction. 'You know who he is?'

'Yes.' She nodded, her interest pricking up sharply. 'He directed *Starfire*.'

'Right. You saw the British Film Society awards on television?' he asked. 'Best picture, best script, best musical score. Quite a haul.'

Chris nodded. 'It was a superb film.'

'Was it?' He gave her one of those dry, ironical looks, but passed no comment on her judgement. 'Successful British film-directors are always very big news. I want you to fix an interview with him. Any slant you like; I trust you to come up with something original. I don't know which house he's staying in, but I'm sure you'll be able to find out.'

'One of the estate agents will know,' she mused, more to herself than to him. This assignment was a lot closer to her heart—and her expression told him that quite clearly!

Unexpectedly, a half-smile creased one side of his mouth. 'I thought that would be more your scene than Ransome Street. I may be just a successful streetfighter, Chris, but I know my instincts are right. See what you can do on both stories, hmm?'

She found herself nodding wearily, thoroughly bamboozled. That 'Chris' had been deliberately thrown in to soften her up. And as for his being nothing more than a successful streetfighter, the briefest glance at what he'd done with the *Herald* so far gave the lie to that.

'I don't seem to have much alternative, do I?' she shrugged.

'You could always refuse,' he invited smoothly.

'That might be a novel experience for both of us,' she said ironically. 'Maybe I should try it. Who knows, it might even get me the sack?'

He looked up sharply. 'You sound as though you almost mean that.'

'Maybe I almost do.'

'I need you,' he said in a threatening voice, as though that were the most compelling reason in the world for her to stay.

'I don't think you do.' She looked out of the window at the view of the winding river, grey in the winter light. Ignoring the ominous descent of his brow, she went on, 'Maybe it would be easier all round if you changed me for someone else. Someone more—shall we say attuned to your way of looking at things.'

'Are you telling me that you're too emotionally involved with this newspaper to work under me?'

The direct question unsettled her. 'I—I don't know...'

He stared at her with glittering eyes for a moment. 'Well, you'd better find out, hadn't you?' he said bluntly. He picked up the discreet ivory telephone and growled, 'Olivia? Get me Bob Jennings and Tom Shoals, please.'

Her cue to exit stage left and reappear after two acts with a brilliant story in her arms.

'Right,' she said heavily to no one in particular, and walked out, leaving him giving orders down the line.

The noise of the newsroom enfolded her again as she walked out. She paused momentarily to look across the long, crowded room. It was a scene as familiar to her as her own image, the orderly confusion of desks, keyboards and telephones that was the true, beating heart of the newspaper.

Yet there was something indefinably different about the newsroom these days. Whether it was the heightened activity, or whether it was the green computer-screens that now glowed among the cluttered desks, or whether it was just the fact that collars and ties had given way to the smart casuals that Nash permitted, the newsroom had changed radically from her father's time.

It was hard not to feel nostalgia for those dear, dead days of slightly shabby gentility and financial gloom.

Nash had swept through the building like the advance guard of some highly developed alien civilisation, ordering the steam-age technology of her father's era to be replaced with the latest micro-circuitry, walls to be painted five shades lighter, everything hustled into a state of ultra-efficient modernity.

And he'd done exactly the same with the *Herald* itself. In the last two years of her father's time, the *Herald* had shrunk from a daily to a twice-weekly, and there had even been plans to bring it out once weekly. Nash had very definitely turned it back into a daily, a *commercial* daily, the sort of newspaper her father would have been incapable of producing in a million years.

It was bigger, brighter, more eye-catching than ever before, from the Monday game of bingo, with its big cash prizes, to the Friday colour supplement.

Chris knew that the rumour about Nash wanting to introduce a page three girl was patently untrue, yet such a suggestion would not have astonished her. The man had a razor-edged instinct for what would sell. Even his editorials reflected that; they were brilliant, incisive, and—though she hated to admit it—formidably well-informed. They caught the thrust of public opinion and gave it a hard edge of clarity. The readers loved them.

But the staid old paper of her father's and grandfather's day had been transformed for ever. She knew what they would have called the new product. *The banner press.* An old-fashioned, snobbish phrase, reflecting all their contempt for the kind of conspicuous journalism Nash represented.

Yet the accounts were showing their first profits in years. For the first time in years, too, the *Herald* was publishing enough copies to cover the bills. The distribution and advertising departments were rushed off their feet; two extra photographers had been employed; and the junior reporters hurried around with shining eyes, agreeing with each other that it was all very wonderful.

Crude? Nash was as brutally efficient as a flicknife, and about as sentimental.

She turned into her own tiny office, the one that had belonged to her father. Though now a pleasant shade of pale blue with matching wall-to-wall carpet, and ornamented with a potted fig-tree she considered ridiculously huge, it still reminded her so strongly of that loveable man...

Six months ago, Chris's father had died suddenly. Like his father before him, he had been the Herald's editor-owner all his life. His demise, and the consequent death-duties, had brought the paper's long-tottering finances down with a mighty crash around their ears. She had barely had time to bury her father, and come to terms with her grief when the accountants had confronted her with the steadily burgeoning crisis.

The bank, concerned about its debenture, had lost confidence in the paper. In their opinion, the Herald had only one option—to go into receivership immediately.

Chris hadn't known whether to feel despair or relief. At twenty-six, she'd recognised that she was not equipped either to edit or manage the Herald. She was just too inexperienced, despite her intimate involvement with the paper. Given another ten years of her father's tutelage, another decade of experience—maybe. But right then, the idea was not feasible.

That was the point at which Nash Canfield's presence had first made itself felt, like the sound of distant thunder. Their gloom turned miraculously into optimism, the accountants had brought her the hint that Someone—note the capital S—was interested in buying the *Lancashire Herald*.

She would never forget that first meeting with Nash Canfield. He'd filled her with a mixture of hope and terror. He'd seemed really capable of doing what she herself knew she could never do single-handed—of refloating the *Herald*, and making it pay. Of saving the jobs of the fifty or more staff, some of them people she'd known since childhood, all of them colleagues to whom she felt a strong sense of duty...

So she'd sold out to him. Or rather, the bank had sold out to him, with her blessing, because by then they'd been the real owners. All that had been hers had been the name. Nash had bought the *Herald*'s assets, lock, stock and printing press. He owned this building, and the warehouse in St John's Lane. He owned the machines and the fleets of distribution and staff vehicles. He even owned the contracts under which most of the staff worked.

At that point, her own position had become more than a little anomalous... But Nash had been quite categorical about his wish that she should stay on the staff.

Under her father, she had been a special reporter, a kind of Girl-Friday post that had been designed to allow her to circulate and learn as much about running the *Herald* as possible—against the possibility that she might, one far-off day, inherit her father's mantle.

Nash, clearly, had seen all this, and had thought out an alternative very carefully. He had offered her the chance to edit the newly set up Wednesday Review. Giving her semi-executive status, but clearly removed from the real seat of power, it was an honourable compromise. He'd also asked her to chair the editorial consultative committee, which had a lot less clout than the formal name suggested. As editor of the Wednesday pages, her brief would be to produce something as outward-going, and as involved in the life of the town, as humanly possible.

She accepted, and so far the results had been very promising. She'd just successfully brought to a close a campaign to raise a very large sum of money to buy equipment for the local children's hospital, and in the summer they had organised a fun run that had brought together almost six hundred townswomen from all walks of life. It wasn't the sort of journalism her father had brought her up to do, but it kept her very busy indeed...

Except that Nash Canfield was the alligator in the pool. Sometimes it seemed to her that there was more alligator than pool. She had regretted the initial enthusiasm which had allowed her to let him talk her into staying on a thousand times. But at that point, she'd still believed he would value her opinion, despite the fact that she would at best have only an advisory status. She had felt, out of some misplaced altruism, that her remaining on might act as a check on Nash, protecting the staff from any excesses the new manager might run to.

Also, in the stunned aftermath of Dad's fatal heart attack, she just hadn't had anywhere else to go. Leaving the *Herald* had seemed inconceivable...

But she should have left, then, cutting all her losses, before all her hope in the future had been turned to bitterness at seeing Nash Canfield's aggressive, thrusting figure in her father's place. Increasingly, she had been aware of an acute sense of loss these days. Not just that she'd lost the family newspaper to Nash, but that the old *Herald*, with its sixty years of tradition, was steadily being lost to the world for ever.

Nash's dark presence was overshadowing her life until she felt like—what was that repulsive image?

'The toad under the harrow,' she murmured to herself with a wry smile. That was the way he made you feel. He was just too abrasive, too aggressive. After a lifetime with this newspaper, it was very hard to see everything transformed around her. She couldn't help resisting the man wherever possible—as she'd done five minutes ago. Fighting to stop herself from becoming a mere rubber stamp, used by Nash to put a gloss on his intentions.

If she kept arguing with him, sooner or later she was really going to land up with the sack. And then he would do exactly what he wanted with the *Herald*.

There was something about him that would have antagonised her under any circumstances, something personal. Something that couldn't be defined, a kind of challenge that Nash presented her with, something that crackled like electricity between them.

She didn't want to go on like this much longer, not in this constant state of tension with him. Leaving the *Herald* was no longer as inconceivable as it had once seemed. And there was a traditional, honourable way out. London. Her years at a provincial reporter's desk, plus her family background in newspaper publishing, would make her an attractive proposition to a London paper...

Jean Symmonds's knock at her door interrupted Chris's gloomy train of thought.

'Thought you were back. Here's the usual.' She put the pile of copy on Chris's desk. Doubling as roving reporter and copy-taster, Jean was the mainstay of the Wednesday Review, partly because of her abiding friendship with Chris. She had always been one of her father's favourites. Her untidy chestnut hair gave her a scatty air that belied her orderly mind, and Chris was very fond of her. Right now, her bony face was alight with gossip waiting to be communicated. 'You'll never guess what *I* saw last night.'

'Try me,' Chris smiled.

'Our revered leader kissing Miss Claws in his office!'

'You're joking,' Chris said. 'Nash?'

'I am not joking. Klaus looked as though she was going to eat him!'

'I can't say I find it incredible,' Chris said wonderingly, her amethyst-grey eyes darkening. The *Herald*'s advertising manager was a very good-looking brunette in her early thirties. Known to all and sundry as 'Miss Claws', she was well known to have a discerning appetite for rich and powerful men. And Anita's whole being had been focused on Nash, with an intensity obvious to everyone, from the very start.

'But in Nash's *office*? Are you sure they weren't just discussing an advertisement or something?'

'I'm not an idiot.' Jean sniffed. 'I just poked my head round the door, and there they were. I shot out again in a hurry, I can tell you.'

'Blast that woman!' Chris said with unexpected vehemence. 'She's been chasing him from the moment he arrived here. And if he falls for her routine, then he's even more misguided than I thought he was.'

'Nash? Misguided?'

'Unless he's just not too fussy about his playmates,' Chris added bitchily. With Jean, she could say things she wouldn't dream of airing abroad. She had known Jean long enough to be able to confide her more private thoughts to her. 'I thought he had taste! Though come to think of it, he's probably just unscrupulous enough to do it.'

'She's very pretty. All that lovely chestnut hair...'

'She's a man-eating shark. And as for him——' Chris's oval face soured. 'He's so repulsive sometimes that it's quite a pleasure to hate him.'

Jean smiled. 'Well, I certainly don't hate him!'

'You don't have to work with him every day,' Chris said moodily, still thinking about Anita. 'I do.'

'Poor thing!'

'It's all very well for you to smile. I really wish he wouldn't keep *consulting* me about things. It's such a useless charade!'

'He respects your opinion. You're Sam Yardley's daughter.'

'He doesn't respect a single thing I say! Every time I contradict him, he just gives me a lecture about why I'm wrong, and he's right...'

'Then he must be grooming you.'

'What for?' Chris scorned.

'I don't understand you,' Jean smiled. 'Most other women would jump at the chance of working with Nash Canfield.'

'You like the man?' Chris challenged.

'I like his editorials,' Jean admitted. 'He hits damned hard, and he always hits the things that I hate most.' Glancing at Chris's expression, Jean added quickly, 'Of course, he doesn't have your father's balanced, educated viewpoint, but...'

'He's a demagogue,' Chris finished, with an edge to her voice.

'In the best possible sense. Also,' Jean said dreamily, 'he's rather a magnificent animal. You can just imagine

him sweeping you over his shoulder. I rather envy Miss
Claws...'

'Well I don't,' Chris snapped.

'You're too wrapped in fighting him to see it,' Jean
said with a smile. 'It's that dark, brooding sensuality of
his. Anyway, what's got you so anti-Nash this morning?'

'Don't remind me,' Chris sighed. 'The Wednesday
page is going to Ransome Street.'

'How exciting!'

'That wasn't quite my reaction,' Chris said irritatedly.
'I tried to tell him that it just didn't fit with the *Herald*'s
status in this town, but I don't think he can see beyond
the distribution-figures.'

'Hmm.' Jean smiled. 'It certainly doesn't fit with the
sort of journalism your father stood for. But it's going
to make a splash all right.'

'I don't think Nash Canfield gives a damn about the
past tradition of the *Herald*,' Chris said. 'And raw com-
mercialism's only part of it. Lately, I've been feeling
more and more that he bought the paper out of sheer
egotism, to have a mouthpiece for his own opinions.
After all,' she said drily, 'having your own paper's the
ultimate ego-trip to that sort of man, isn't it? I mean,
think of his crusading editorials, hitting out at things
that annoy him—what better way to pump up your self-
opinion?'

'Nash doesn't need pumping up. And as for Ransome
Street—well, I mean, it's like the emperor's new clothes,
isn't it? Everyone knows what goes on, but no one dares
say anything about it. I think it's a marvellous topic.
Seriously, don't you?'

'It hardly matters what I think,' Chris said with a
businesslike air. 'Ours not to reason why, ours but to
do and die. I daren't argue any more. Nash would tear

me limb from limb. He seems to get a positive pleasure out of tormenting me.'

'Of course he does,' Jean smiled. 'I think he rather goes for you.'

'What nonsense,' Chris retorted, taken aback. 'He feels as cold about me as I do about him!'

'Really?' Jean wore an odd smile. 'I think you're rather his type.'

'I couldn't be any less his type!' Irritably, she was aware of her cheeks flushing. 'He suspects anyone who's got a regular education, and I went to an exclusive school. He simply detests the old-fashioned way of running the *Herald*, and I'm all for it. On top of which, he's a woman-hater, and I'm a woman!'

Jean studied her friend. Christine Yardley's was a neat, lithe body, blessed with long, beautiful legs and elegant lines. Any impression of delicacy wouldn't have been accurate, though; Chris was as springy as a high-stepping doe. She had her mother's full mouth, but the hint of passion mixed with melancholy was all her own; and the amethyst grey of her eyes was as striking as the natural silver-blonde of her long, silky hair.

'If there's one thing Nash admires, my dear Chris, it's intelligence. And you have a great deal of that. Added to which, you're a very good journalist, and that's quite a different thing. Besides——' She held up a hand to stem Chris's retort. '—he seems to bring out the best in you. You've blossomed, as a person and as a journalist. The past six months on the Wednesday Review have been the most exciting period in my whole career.' Not pausing long enough for Chris to get any kind of reply in edgeways, Jean started passing the copy across to Chris. 'This is a report just in from the Press Association about breast cancer. Sally wants to know whether you think

an item in the medical column is called for. And there
are two short stories in from local writers, one of them
really quite good...'

Pushing her conflict with Nash to the darker recesses
of her mind, Chris concentrated on the mass of information that Jean had assembled for her attention.
Somehow, all this jumble of facts, pictures and prose
would have to be processed into the Wednesday Review
over the next few days.

It wasn't until Jean had left, almost an hour later,
that her friend's words returned to her mind. Had she
really expanded under Nash's editorship? Chris shook
her head slowly. She found that very hard to believe.
Jean's obvious attraction towards Nash Canfield had
struck her several times before. She knew that she herself
would never think of Nash in those terms; she disliked
him far too much. She didn't see him as a man—more
as a potentially devastating elemental force, better
avoided if possible, to be faced only when strictly
necessary.

*I think you're rather his type.*

Some women might go weak at the knees in the
presence of that rather overpowering virility, but Chris
Yardley wasn't one of them. The qualities she admired
in a man were creativity, tolerance, sensitivity. Nash
Canfield didn't have an ounce of the last two, and as
for the first—well, if you could call a volcano creative,
then you might apply the word to Nash, but not
otherwise.

It was damnable, the way he got her back up. Sometimes he made her so angry she could scarcely think—
and things like the news about Anita Klaus didn't help
in the slightest. Hearing Jean's bit of gossip had really
upset and sickened her. Everyone knew he was attractive

to women. Why the hell did he have to prove it? And why with that ambitious, vulgar little serpent Anita?

Damn him for kissing Anita. *Damn* him!

With an effort, she turned her attention to the assignment she'd been given.

Duncan Anderson was a very gifted director. *Starfire*, his sixth film, was a decidedly erotic love story. Starring a very beautiful and hitherto little-known young actress, it told the story of a young woman's unsuccessful marriage, and her attempts to find fulfilment with several other lovers. The three Film Society awards had confirmed critical enthusiasm for the film.

The only problem she foresaw was that Anderson himself was a somewhat private person. He hadn't been present, for example, to receive his award—Zara Zoffany, *Starfire*'s principal actress, had done that for him. She would have to play it with sensitivity.

It was certainly a glamorous assignment, and the first thing on the agenda was to track him down. Within minutes, though, a good friend in a local estate agency had supplied the answer she wanted. She rang the number, but there was no reply. Well, at least she'd located him; she'd ring back later.

As she put the phone down a deep hum, more felt than heard, rose up through the floor under Chris's feet. To her, it had always been the most exciting of sounds— the deep rumble of the presses starting up on the ground floor, getting ready to print the first 'evening' edition— actually, an early afternoon edition. In the courtyard outside, the fleet of vans would soon be assembling to get the first warm bundles out to the distribution-points, and from there to newsagents across the county.

It wasn't the *Herald* her grandfather had founded. And it wasn't being run by her father any more. But at least it was still alive...

Soothed by the familiar vibration, which she'd known and loved since childhood, she thrust Nash Canfield out of her mind, and picked up her telephone.

'Hello, switchboard. Can you get me Professor Myra Matthews, Department of Social Studies at the University, please.' She pulled her pad towards her, and wrote RANSOME STREET at the top, in capitals. Then she leaned forward, shifting into gear. 'Hello. Professor Matthews? It's Chris Yardley here, from the *Herald*. I wonder if you could spare me some time today or tomorrow? It's about Ransome Street.'

# CHAPTER TWO

THE pleasant voice that answered her telephone call the next morning was lightly accented with a Scots brogue.

'Duncan Anderson speaking.'

'Good morning, Mr Anderson. My name's Christine Yardley, from the *Herald*.'

'Oh, yes?' he replied coolly.

'I'm sorry to intrude,' she said. 'I'm the editor of the Wednesday Review, which is our women's section. I wondered whether you'd give me an interview while you're in Lancashire, for the arts page? I'd appreciate it very much.'

There was a slight pause. 'I didn't think anyone knew I was here. Your information's very good, Mrs Yardley.'

'It's Miss Yardley,' she corrected politely. 'And your presence here is big news, Mr Anderson. I'd be very grateful...'

There was another pause, and then a sigh. 'Well, I suppose I'm free tomorrow afternoon.'

'Wonderful!' she enthused. 'Would two o'clock suit you?'

Chris could sense his mental shrug. 'I suppose so.'

'And would you mind if I brought a photographer with me?' she ventured.

This time the reaction was not so positive.

'I'd rather not, actually. I do come up here for privacy, you know.'

Quit while you're ahead, she told herself. 'Well, I look forward to tomorrow afternoon, then,' she said pleasantly. 'Thank you, Mr Anderson.'

'Bye.'

She put the receiver down with a sense of relief. That had been painless enough. In the mean time, she could get down to evaluating the mass of information Myra Matthews had given her yesterday.

She was giving the Ransome Street problem her full attention, now, and it was bigger than she'd imagined. There were some very fascinating side-issues starting to appear already. If her instincts were right, there was going to be enough interest in the story to generate a two-section investigation, with an opinion poll, and maybe a defence by one of the prostitutes themselves as a spin-off.

Ugly stuff, ugly enough to give her a shiver of distaste. But Nash had been right. It would definitely whip up both interest and sales—and that would please *him*, at any rate, whatever damage it did to the *Herald*'s reputation...

Over the course of the day, the spell of unseasonal sunshine gave way to a real winter blizzard. The fierce weather battered the *Herald* building all day, hail following snow, turning eventually to enduring sleet.

Chris was deep in work by the time the banging of doors outside announced that five-thirty had come round, and people were starting to leave. A skeleton staff of copy-takers was coming in to man the phones and teleprinters overnight. The final 'late' edition of the *Herald* was being printed, and it was as though the entire building had let its sense of urgency out in a long, tired sigh.

Acknowledging her own weariness, Chris made a final note on the pad at her side, and leaned back in her chair with a yawn. The snow was still sweeping across the distant river, and the prospect of trudging home through the foul weather was hardly appealing. Her father's Rover was parked in the garage at home. She seldom used it, anyway, but she was wishing she hadn't decided to get the bus today, of all days.

She sat up with a start as her door swung open to admit Nash, carrying a large, flat object wrapped in brown paper.

'Good,' he grunted, shooting her one of his glittering black looks, 'you're still here.'

'Still earning my keep,' she said with well-practised sweetness. The silk suit which hugged his powerful shoulders was spattered with snow. 'Been shopping?'

'You could say that.' He towered over her, making her office suddenly seem a size too small. If she could read that rugged face, it was wearing an expression of satisfaction. 'How's the Anderson assignment going?'

'I tracked him down this morning,' she said with just a hint of smugness. 'I'm going out to the gorge to interview him tomorrow afternoon.'

He grunted. 'And the Ransome Street business?'

'Shaping up,' she acknowledged. 'I've spoken to several people today, and it looks as though public opinion is coming up to the boil. There's definitely going to be a lot of feedback to the first set of stories, enough, I'd guess, to warrant spreading the investigation over two issues.'

His eyes warmed. 'Good,' was all he said; but Chris felt her whole body tingle with the impact of his approval. Why did he affect her so acutely?

He hefted the big, flat package on to her desk. 'I've been waiting a long time for this, Yardley.' She watched in puzzlement as he tore the brown-paper wrapping off.

Revealed was a painting. Chris slid her glasses off to stare at the powerfully modern composition: an explosion of white light, fragmented and dazzling, against an arc of deepest midnight blue. It was almost bright enough to hurt the eyes, a painting that had an immediate, unforgettable impact.

'What is it?' she asked in awe.

'Supporting local artists is one of the duties of a newspaper editor,' he smiled. 'It's a Roger Gauld. One of his best.'

The painting wasn't her taste. A work of genius it might be, but she preferred her décor a little less demanding. 'Very nice,' she said.

'I'm glad you approve.' He hefted the large canvas and held it against the wall. 'About here, I'd say.'

'In my office?' Chris felt her expression curdle. 'Here?'

'Oh, don't thank me,' he said, tilting his dark head to admire the work. 'You deserve only the best.'

Appalled at the prospect of having the painting in her office, she scrabbled frantically through her vocabulary bin for a polite refusal. 'Isn't it a little too—er—a little too *big* for this office, Nash?'

'Well, well.' His expression could have meant anything from tolerant contempt to ironic amusement. 'I never suspected you of possessing such a drab soul, Yardley.'

'In a modern art gallery, it would be *lovely*,' she said with an effort at sincerity. 'But in here it's a bit like Rachmaninov at full volume.'

'Exactly,' he said, looking at the picture through thick, dark lashes. 'Someone has to improve your taste. You can't spend the rest of your life training your personality around paintings of kittens playing with balls of wool.'

'I do rather prefer representational art,' she said in a tight little voice, her temper straining at its moorings after the kittens jibe. He had been very scornful about the way the office had been furnished previously. 'Dreadfully old-fashioned, I know, but there it is.'

His eyes were mocking. 'You ought to be flattered, you little philistine. Give it time.' He glanced at his watch as though she hadn't spoken. 'It's getting on for six. Come on, I'll take you home.'

'I'd rather take the bus,' she assured him, wishing to God she could win an argument against him for once in her life.

'There's a blizzard out there,' he pointed out. 'And besides, there's a bus-drivers' strike.'

'Oh, no!' She peered out of the window in dismay, to see a familiar red shape trundle through the slushy traffic down below. 'There are still buses running,' she accused suspiciously.

'But not to Woodside. Buses to Woodside are cancelled.' She stared at his tanned, expressionless face. Was he teasing her? 'Oh, come on,' he said explosively as she hesitated. 'You're not that terrified, are you?'

'What should I be terrified of?' she said defensively.

'Of spending a car-ride alone with me.'

She thought of Anita Klaus, and felt a squirt of venom along her veins. 'No, I'm not terrified,' she said in a carefully balanced voice, scooping up her coat with suppressed tension. 'I'm ready to go.'

His normally imperious mouth was twitching at the corners as he ushered her through the emptying

newsroom and into the deserted passage. 'Tell me something,' he commanded, 'when are you going to forgive
me for making the *Herald* pay?'

She gave him a sour look, and he took her arm, his
laughter deep and sexy. The contact with his hard, warm
body swelled her pulses dizzily as the blood seemed to
rush through her veins. God, he had something. A power,
a magnetism, call it what you will. Sickened to discover
that she wasn't immune, she pulled away from him with
a racing heart. Coal-black eyes as deep as chasms studied
her. 'You're very jumpy.'

'Just playing safe,' she snapped, unwisely.

'Oh?' One eyebrow tilted dangerously. 'What exactly
does that mean?'

'Nothing,' she muttered. If Anita Klaus hadn't been
on her mind, she'd never have said anything so stupid.
But it had been lodged in her thoughts like a poisoned
dart, festering.

'I know that meaningful tone of voice,' he challenged, a whole terrifying octave lower. 'Spit it out.'

'Why should I bother you with my girlish fears and
fancies?' she enquired sweetly. 'Anyway, they say bru-
nettes are flavour of the month.'

That stare was awesome. 'Yardley! You've been
listening to office gossip.'

'I suppose you were really removing a piece of dust
from her eye,' Chris suggested drily.

'No,' he said calmly. 'There wasn't any dust in her
eye. Her need was—shall we say, more personal.'

She couldn't meet his eyes for the pain and anger
inside. 'Well, if you insist on kissing Anita Klaus at the
office, you'll have to put up with office gossip.' Her tone
and expression were icy, but he seemed unimpressed.

They paused to pick up the late edition of the paper from the box in the foyer. The ink was so fresh that it stained Chris's fingers. She unfolded her copy, and stared at the front-page headline. The main news of the day was of a growing national industrial crisis, set to blossom over the next few days. Articles around the main story dealt with the impact the situation was likely to have on local life. The rest of the front-page news was local, the stories continuing over on to pages two and three. A good, interesting front page.

She followed Nash through the driving snow to the sleek green Rolls-Royce Camargue that always stood in his special bay outside the *Herald* building. She flipped through the paper in silence as he eased the luxurious car through the tangled traffic of the town centre, past the cathedral, towards Woodside. As if indifferent to her lack of conversation, he slid a tape into the stereo, and the calm, sweet strains of a Mozart piano concerto filled the leather and walnut interior.

The fact that the concerto was one of her own best-loved favourites only made her smoulder all the more. How could a barbarian like Nash end up choosing the sort of music that spread fingers of ecstasy across her soul?

'Home must be rather empty these days,' he observed laconically, hands sure at the big wheel. 'Do you ever get lonely out there in the sticks?'

'Sometimes,' she said, then regretted the admission immediately.

'You could always sell the house. It would fetch a tidy sum, I'd guess. Then you could move into a flat, closer to the bright lights.'

'I love the house,' she said irritably, folding the paper away. Damn it, everything he said seemed to rub on her nerves! 'I grew up there.'

'Take in a lodger,' he suggested, accelerating blood-thirstily through a gap in the traffic. 'How about me?'

'I think not,' she said tersely. 'I'm not the landlady type.'

'I'm teasing, Yardley.' He hummed along with the slow movement for a while, his voice deep and melodious. 'Loneliness isn't good for a young woman,' he commented, after a while. He sounded about as sympathetic as a hunk of granite. 'You need more fun. Friends, parties, nightclubs.'

'I don't like nightclubs,' she ground out. 'And I have all the friends I want.'

'Including men friends?'

She glanced at his rocky profile sharply. He was getting personal, and it disturbed her. 'That really isn't your business.' Which was obviously water off a duck's back, because Nash merely moved on to another question.

'Of course,' he mused to himself, 'there's your grand-mother. You're very close to her. But your mother's in Shropshire now, isn't she?' And, when Chris nodded, 'See much of her?'

'Now and then,' she said quietly, her eyes turning rainy-grey with melancholy. She hadn't been close to her mother since the protracted divorce battle that had occupied most of her sixteenth year. Her mother, now re-married and living in Shropshire, hadn't even come down for Dad's funeral.

'Now and then,' he repeated, sounding almost as though he pitied her. 'That's hardly a family relationship.'

Chris glanced at him, taken aback at his apparently encyclopaedic curiosity about her life. 'I didn't think your staff interested you this much,' she ventured, tucking one leg under her to turn in the leather seat and face him.

'Not usually,' he commented obliquely. 'But you're something special, aren't you?'

She didn't ask him to elaborate. An elaboration might have been acutely embarrassing, anyway.

'And your stepfather?' he pressed on. 'Does he take an interest?'

'I don't see why he should,' she parried the question.

'Well, if I had a stunningly beautiful daughter living alone, I might take a little notice of her.'

'Charles and Mum have their own life,' she said tiredly. She was past being hurt by their lack of concern for her, not any more.

At the traffic lights he favoured her with a slow glance, then accelerated forward again. 'Do you miss your father badly?'

'I don't really want to talk about it,' Chris said, coolly drawing the line, 'if you don't mind.'

Nash smiled, showing those excellent teeth again. 'I don't mind. You should never be offended at anything I do or say. I just wonder whether it galls you to see me sitting in your father's seat, so to speak.'

'Of course not,' she said, too quickly.

'Even though I'm changing his life's work?'

'A newspaper isn't a static thing,' she said tonelessly. 'It has to change and adapt if it's to survive.'

He laughed softly. Nash was far too intelligent to miss the fact that she was quoting his own words back at him verbatim, with an experienced reporter's memory. 'Then why do I get the impression that you're working against me, instead of with me?'

'I'm doing my best to work *for* you,' she said pointedly.

He picked that nuance up, too. For a tough man, he was astonishingly good at picking up even her most delicate hints. 'But I won't let you make a full contribution?' he suggested. 'I ignore your efforts to stop me from changing the *Herald*. Right?'

'You're making this newspaper pay for the first time in years,' Chris said, her tone careful. 'We're all behind you. But sometimes it might be appropriate to give consideration to members of staff who have, shall we say, a little more experience of local conditions.'

'Who have, shall we say, a lemming-like desire to see the *Herald* sink back into the obscurity it so richly deserved,' he retorted. But he didn't seem particularly annoyed, and by his expression he was waiting for more.

'I agree with you——' She stopped, corrected herself. 'We *all* agree with you that there's a place for the *Herald* in this town. An important place. But not necessarily as a huge commercial success.'

'As a weekend gossip-rag?' he suggested. 'Reporting the results of last weekend's livestock shows?'

'As a *local* paper,' she said, emphasising the word. They were rehearsing an argument which had been thrashed out several times already in different contexts. In her own mind, she saw it as chip-chipping away at a granite slab. Eventually, you might get somewhere. Eventually. 'It's a mistake to think that the influence of the *Herald* can be measured in circulation figures,' she said. 'People pass copies around, from person to person and from family to family. They value it for the solid facts in it. Solid facts and solid names.' She looked at him. 'The *Herald* has maintained a very fine tradition in this town, Nash. It's important. People rely on it to help them form sound opinions. They like it because it mentions their names, and prints photographs of them.'

He grunted, but didn't interrupt.

'My father never bothered about sensationalism,' she went on, her voice just a little unsteady now. 'That didn't mean he couldn't raise hell if he thought something needed raising hell about. But he respected people, and people respected him. That's what local journalism is all about.'

'Quite a speech,' he said softly. 'How much of that is Sam Yardley, and how much is your own?'

'You never knew him,' she answered, just as quietly. 'Maybe that's a pity. Traditionally——'

'You know,' he muttered, 'that's a word I'm growing sick of the sound of.'

'Traditionally,' she repeated, 'people have bought the *Herald* for certain specific reasons. You're asking them to buy it for very different reasons.'

He growled. 'Well, we're going to break with *tradition*. We're going to make the *Herald* the most exciting rag in this county.' He swung the big car around the crescent. 'Look, I respect your opinions, of course I do. And I like to think that I'm continuing the best part of the *Herald* tradition—in my own way. But times have changed, girl. Costs have risen enormously, you know that.'

'Yes, but——'

'Your father made some very serious mistakes with the paper,' he said harshly. 'Cutting back to two issues a week was particularly stupid. It meant that the presses were only being used eight times a month, reducing the

*Herald*'s profitability even further. It wasn't costing much less to print, and he was selling far fewer copies.'

Chris sat in a bitter silence. When he attacked her dead father like this, it made her really hate him. Who on earth was he to call Dad stupid?

'Selling copies is what it's all about,' he went on. 'That comes before selling advertising, or anything else. We just don't have any choice. This paper still isn't out of the red. To make it succeed, we need to expand our readership rapidly and permanently. We *have* to compete with the nationals. I know you hate the bingo and the colour supplement—and I suspect you secretly even despise your own Wednesday Review.' She looked down, ashamed of his insight. 'But they all sell copies,' he said, more gently. 'Surely you understand that?'

'Well, I may not have your iron grasp of high finance,' she told him in a voice like the finest wine vinegar. 'But then I do have the slight advantage of having lived here all my life, and having seen my family run the *Herald* ever since I was a baby.'

'Spare me the superior tone,' he growled.

Chris changed tack. Nash had savaged his way to the top via the streets, and was well known to detest being patronised by the socially advantaged. 'Nash, I do have some insights into the situation. In my opinion, it would be a very serious mistake to try and push the *Herald* too far.'

'Too far?' He snorted, even more bull-like. 'I haven't even pushed it out of its grave yet!'

'Maybe it should have been left to lie there.' She folded her arms, her eyes bright with anger. 'Maybe the correct approach would have been to contract the paper, not expand it.'

'The correct approach is to make the *Herald* make money,' Nash retorted brusquely. 'I'm not asking you to sell your souls, for God's sake. I'm asking you to have a little vision. To work a lot harder. To reach after something beyond your grasp.'

'Like prostitution around Ransome Street?'

'Oh, come.' There was a hint of brute muscle under the Savile Row tailoring. 'If you want me to take the Wednesday Review away from you, just say so.'

'I don't,' she said quietly.

'Good. Your father spent his life pouring money into a bottomless well. It ruined him. It *killed* him. The key to a successful newspaper is a healthy circulation, and there's no other way.'

'So you keep telling us.' But there were other viewpoints. Her eyes, a luminous shade between grey and violet, were bitter. She dropped the topic, recognising a dead-end when she saw one, and sat in silence, feeling all twisted up inside. Being with Nash tangled her emotions painfully, like the tangled shrouds of a parachute, and with the same end result—a very nasty fall. He just wasn't amenable to persuasion. Maybe it was time she looked around for another job, and cut Nash, the *Herald*, and everything connected with them out of her life...

He drove on in a thoughtful silence until the Rolls was turning down Woodside Avenue, a street of solid, attractive houses facing the dark mass of the forest.

'Just drop me at the corner,' she invited.

'It's no trouble.'

'Here will do fine,' she insisted.

'Are you afraid the neighbours will think I'm your sugar-daddy?' he smiled, driving down the avenue anyway.

'You're not old' enough to be my sugar-daddy,' she said without thinking.

'Your lover, then.'

She cursed herself for flushing at his wickedly amused glance. 'Whatever. Either way, my reputation couldn't stand the knock.'

'You're too young to have a reputation.' The age gap between them probably accounted for a lot of their mutual tension. Although there were streaks of distinguished grey at Nash's temples, his hair was thick and dark. The taut power of his body might make you guess at a very athletic thirty; but the deeply-incised lines around his eyes and mouth put at least five years on that.

As soon as he brought the car to a halt outside her green gate, she opened the door hastily and swung her long, beautiful legs out. Iron fingers bit into her wrist, pinning her before she could escape. 'Not so fast,' he growled.

'Oh, silly me,' she exclaimed, hoping the irony would cover her fluttering nerves at the contact. 'You'll be wanting your petrol money.'

'Don't push the schoolgirl jokes too far,' he warned, eyes dark as midnight on hers. She dropped her gaze, embarrassed. His eyes drifted deliberately down her figure. 'It's high time we harnessed your full potential,' he said, as if to himself. 'You've been wasted on the desert air unseen for too long.'

'I like a quiet life,' she had to smile.

'You're too valuable,' he said flatly. 'And by the way, I'm not too fussy about what my staff wear, but are tight pants and a T-shirt really appropriate?'

She got out irritably. The tailored linen trousers and cotton blouse she'd worn today were quite smart enough for ordinary office wear. 'I'll wear a silk dress tomorrow,' she said shortly, through the open door.

'No,' he decided. 'You're the sort of girl who looks ravishing in jeans, but a little coltish in a silk dress.'

He reached out and closed the heavy door for her. The Rolls purred up the street, and she barged through her gate and into the house. Damn Canfield, she thought, cuddling the delighted cat. He knew just how to make her jump.

In her cream and white bedroom—no pictures of playful kittens in sight, drat you, Nash—she hauled off her blouse and trousers and hopped around the room trying to pull on corduroys and a woolly jumper at the same time. It was past six, and she was due at her grandmother's for dinner.

She checked herself in the mirror. She'd always been blessed with an elegant figure, satin-skinned and slender. She'd never been heavy; willowy was the word. Her hips were just wide enough to be fully feminine, and she'd long since stopped worrying that her breasts might be too small. Men looked, and when she went bra-less, they stared.

And there was something about her figure, a neatness, a unity, that made all her movements flow gracefully and easily. That innate grace could transform her good looks into true beauty on occasions. It would not have been surprising if Nash—as she now and then suspected—was sexually attracted to her. Except that Nash's feelings for her was one of the areas she dwelled on least in her mind. Even now, she thrust any such notion out of her thoughts with vehemence.

'Come on, Yardley,' she growled in a contralto imitation of her boss's gravelly voice, 'get moving, girl.'

* * *

Chris was at her grandmother's house by six-thirty. The old place was always spotless, all the antique furniture gleaming.

'You look so lovely, Chrissie.'

Chris kissed her grandmother's cheek. 'So do you, Gran. What's for dinner?'

She smiled, so like Chris's father that it almost made her wince. 'Wait and see. How's work?'

'Exhausting. But it keeps me busy.'

'I'm glad to hear it.' She shot Chris a bright glance. 'How's Mr Canfield?'

'Don't ask,' she said ruefully. 'Every hour I can spend out of Nash Canfield's company is a happy hour as far as I'm concerned.' She passed her grandmother the late edition of the *Herald* she'd brought from work. 'The latest bee in his bonnet is an investigation of the ladies of the night along Ransome Street.'

'The prostitutes?' Dorothy put on her glasses to study the front page. 'Interesting,' she nodded, totally unshocked. 'High time someone tackled the question. I shall enjoy reading that.' Chris's irritated snort made her look up. 'Are you still thinking of resigning?'

'More than ever!'

Gran picked up a magazine, and folded it open. 'This article might interest you.'

Chris studied the article, which was headlined 'Canfield On The Move'. The black-and-white photo didn't do justice to Nash's compelling looks, but the text—'one of the most forceful and thrusting personalities on the business scene'—seemed to have caught his character accurately. The main topic of the article was Nash's achievement with the *Herald*.

'He has transformed a sleepy provincial newspaper into a force to be reckoned with, even in Fleet Street.'

'How dare they?' she cried indignantly. 'The *Herald* was never sleepy!'

'Yes, it was. I like the new *Herald*,' the old lady said serenely. 'It's interesting. And I like Canfield's editorials. He doesn't pull his punches, and he's not afraid to take on any injustice he sees. That's good.'

'Yes, but——'

'This is a stodgy old town. It needs waking up. And the paper's doing better than it's ever done.'

'Oh, he's very good at making money,' Chris acknowledged irritably. 'Profit comes first and last.'

'Not an unreasonable approach.'

'No, it isn't unreasonable. It's just so alien to me.'

'Is that why you're so eager to leave a very good job, with an excellent salary and excellent prospects?' Gran smiled.

Chris shook her head, knowing Gran would never understand how ambivalent she felt. 'It isn't all roses. Nash is very, very hard to work for at times. It's not easy to watch him transform the *Herald* into something utterly different, breaking every rule that Dad ever made.'

'Nothing is ever all roses,' Dorothy said patiently. 'At twenty-six, you must have realised that, Chris. Nash Canfield has offered the *Herald* a marvellous chance to survive and prosper——'

'And I should learn to live with it,' Chris cut in. 'Yeah, I was being told that only yesterday.'

'Then get rid of your misplaced loyalty to Sam.'

'Dad was a great journalist——'

'Sam's dead.' Gran's expression was sad. 'And Sam's ways are dead with him. Your allegiance is to Nash

Canfield now, not to your father. And Nash Canfield is going to be a greater journalist than your father ever was.'

This time, Chris was really shocked. *'Gran!'*

'Come on.' Her grandmother was terminating the conversation. 'Let's eat.' Chris knew that look on her face; Gran didn't want any more discussion to dilute the impact of what she'd just said. She was supposed to digest, and learn!

With a sigh, she rose to follow.

# CHAPTER THREE

IT WAS probably the cold weather, but also possibly because Chris had barely used the car since her father's death. Either way, the Rover refused point-blank to start the next morning.

When the battery started to show signs of going flat, she abandoned it in the garage, and hurried to get the bus. It was still snowing, and the journey in to work was anything but pleasant. Under the fawn trenchcoat, her clothes were mainly light linen, and she was freezing.

When she finally got in to the *Herald*, the newsroom was buzzing with the overnight political developments. The threat of a major industrial wrangle was steadily entangling the government, the opposition, and the unions.

The story was still breaking, and already it was evident that it was going to dominate the evening edition. Through his opened door, Chris caught a glimpse of Nash's six-foot-six figure in conference with Bill Wright, the news editor. She could almost sense the purposeful intentness in the man, the aura of stillness around him despite the confusion of the newsroom.

Wisely, she kept out of everybody's way until lunch time. There was plenty of background reading to go through before she faced Duncan Anderson in the afternoon. He'd had an eventful career.

Hearing the continuing uproar from the newsroom, she felt a stab of envy. People out there were immersed in *real* journalism. Rushing out on assignments, tapping their network of sources, phoning stories in to the copy-takers from call-boxes across the county——

And here she sat, patiently collating her Wednesday Review. She sighed. It was suspiciously like a backwater. But it was journalism, too, of a sort . . .

By noon, most of the senior reporters were either out, or working intently on stories. Noting that Nash's office was empty, probably for the first time all morning, she poked her head through his door.

'My car's broken down,' she announced. 'Can I have a staff car to get out to the gorge?'

Dark eyes met hers. 'If you come all the way in. And ask nicely.'

Reluctantly, she obeyed. '*Please* can I have a staff car?'

Nash rose from behind his desk, an affable expression stitched across his tanned face. He looked stunning in a charcoal suit with a red rose at the lapel, and seeing him took her breath away for a moment. He had . . . *impact*.

'What's wrong with the Rover?' he enquired.

'Probably the cold,' she shrugged. He seemed to know everything about her, even the make of her car. 'I'll get the RAC out this evening, but right now I have to go across country to see Duncan Anderson. I just hope the snowploughs have got out to the secondary roads by now.'

'I hadn't forgotten.' He dangled something bright in front of her. 'Take the Rolls. That should impress Mr Anderson.'

'I'd rather not!'

'Then you'll have to walk,' he said easily. 'All the cars are out. In case you hadn't noticed, the country's teetering on the brink of a national crisis.'

Chris took the keys reluctantly, wondering whether she'd be able to drive Nash's limousine through the bad weather. 'I'll get it back to you as soon as I can,' she promised.

'No rush. I'll be working late. I've a hunch we'll be pulling the presses tonight, anyway.' He surveyed her with all-male attention to the details of her dress. She was wearing pastel shades, which suited her flawless complexion perfectly: a pink linen jacket and grey linen trousers, white silk polo-shirt and silk scarf, plain grey shoes. 'You look ravishing this morning,' he purred, using his husky voice to bring gooseflesh prickling across her skin. 'Trying to seduce Mr Anderson?'

'Just trying to look neat,' she said, with unnecessary stiffness.

'You look very neat. Neat, feminine, cool, and down-right infuriating.' Smoky eyes caressed the sweet oval of her face. 'There's not a great deal of you, but what there is is top-quality stuff.'

'The slave is grateful for the master's notice,' she said coolly.

He looked as though he were considering whether that merited a rebuke. 'You really don't like me, do you, Yardley?'

'I'd say we don't like each other,' she said, keeping it just this side of impertinence as she turned away from him.

'Would you, now?' Iron fingers closed round her wrist to pull her back, as he'd done once before. 'Would you really say that?'

'It's true, isn't it?' But her hand was trembling in his grasp, her mouth unsteady as she tried to smile up into the intensity of those dark eyes, that broodingly passionate mouth. 'We haven't got on since the moment you first walked into this building, Nash.'

'And what would you put that down to?' he asked, velvety menace in his deep voice.

'I—— Chemistry, I suppose,' she faltered.

'Chemistry.' He was still looking down at her, so close that she could smell his skin, the faint tang of very, very expensive aftershave. He reached up slowly to touch her soft cheek with his fingers, his thumb caressing the sensitive satin of her full lower lip. Whether it was the touch or the expression in his eyes, Chris shuddered helplessly, thick lashes drooping down over eyes that had suddenly become soft as grey mist.

Then, realising that they could be seen through the glass panel in his door, she pulled away quickly. In God's name, what was the hold Nash had over her? How could he make her feel like this, turning her, a highly efficient young woman, into a disorganised, quivering mass just by a touch on her lips?

'I'll see you later,' she said shortly, and pushed through the door.

But not before she heard his soft reply. 'I'll be waiting.'

Chris was oddly nervous as she pulled up outside the farmhouse, which commanded a spectacular view of the gorge. She peered through the windscreen at the large stone house, its roof white with snow, then checked her hair and the state of her lightly applied make-up. Then, scooping up her heavy leather shoulder-bag, she made her way up to the house.

The door was opened by a man in a tweed jacket. It was his expression of tension, more than the patrician features themselves, that she recognised from the photographs she'd looked at. Apart from that, he was a handsome man in his forties, with a prematurely lined face, and a mane of dark grey hair. At the sight of her, the creases round his eyes eased slightly.

'Mr Anderson?' she greeted him. 'Hello. I'm Christine Yardley.'

'Come in, come in.' He offered her a warm handshake and a smile that showed good, if crooked, teeth.

The farmhouse was luxuriously appointed. A huge log fire was roaring in the old stone fireplace, and a blast of heat greeted her as he led her into the oak-panelled reception room.

'Let me take your coat,' he offered, reaching for her Burberry. 'My housekeeper's just made tea.'

'Lovely,' she said gratefully. He draped her coat over a hook behind the door, then turned to her, rubbing his hands.

'Shall we talk in here? I find the ambience of this room very... soothing.'

'It's a beautiful room,' she agreed, looking around it, and then at him. 'Have you stayed here before?'

'Oh, many times. I love this part of the world. My family used to come down here for holidays when I was a child. We used to stay in a farmhouse exactly like this one, on the other side of the gorge.' His eyes were light green, his features handsome in the aquiline way quite common in Highland Scots. 'Shall we sit by the fire?'

'Fine.' With some hesitation, she took the taperecorder out of her bag. 'Do you object to my leaving this on?'

'I don't think I'll say anything that much worth preserving,' he said drily, 'but use it by all means.' He held up a hand. 'One condition, Christine, before we start. You give me a ring, preferably before galley-proof stage, and read me the text of your article. If there's anything I object to, I'd like to be able to say so then.'

'Of course.' She nodded, studying the handsome face. 'You seem to know something about newspapers?'

'They fascinate me,' he said simply. 'If I hadn't had the chance of going to the Cinema Arts College, I'd almost certainly have been a journalist.'

'Indeed?' She raised delicate eyebrows. 'Well, that makes an interesting start, anyway!'

'As it happens, I've just been reading an article about your own new editor.' He picked up a copy of that week's *Economist*. 'He seems a fascinating character.'

'He is,' Chris agreed neutrally.

'An interesting situation for you, I would guess,' Anderson went on. 'You're Sam Yardley's daughter, aren't you?'

'You're well informed.' Chris couldn't help smiling.

'Just guesswork.' He was still watching her with those light green eyes. 'It can't be easy seeing your father replaced by a man so very different...' Thankfully, he didn't wait for an answer to that question. 'What's he like? One of these aggressive, ultra-male men? All androgen and high achievement?'

'Well,' Chris hesitated, half-amused by the description, 'that's a little crude. Nash is a very complicated man. He's always about ten steps ahead of you, and he has a brilliant, incisive mind. But yes, he is a high achiever.'

'What's it like working at the new *Herald*?'

'Very stimulating,' she said, and left it at that. But he shook a warning forefinger at her.

'No, no! I really want to know. Before I let you into *my* life, Christine, I want to know a little more about *you*.'

'Well...' She hesitated, rather pleased than otherwise by the great man's interest in her. 'People used to say that Nash had thrown the baby out with the bathwater. But the *Herald*'s performance over the past half-year has been a very effective answer to his critics. It's like...' She hunted for an appropriate image. '...like seeing an old ship rescued from the knacker's yard, stripped down to the bone, and then completely rebuilt. Maybe the new colours are too bright on the eye, and maybe the new materials don't quite match the old patina—but there's no question but that she's a going concern again.'

'And for her crew,' Anderson suggested, 'that means redemption.'

'Yes. That, too.'

The housekeeper came in with tea and biscuits, and Anderson invited her to do the honours.

'You interest me,' he said unexpectedly, as she passed him a teacup. It didn't seem to call for a reply, so she just looked at him enquiringly. 'My experiences with lady journalists haven't always been happy ones. I wouldn't have enjoyed this meeting if you'd turned out to be some grim-faced harridan!'

'Oh, I hope I'm not that,' she smiled.

'I can see that you're not,' he said, stirring his tea. 'To tell the truth, when you said you were an editor, my heart sank. I had a vision of some high-achieving, hard-nosed, masculine woman. That type makes me feel so threatened. Maybe I'm just a chauvinist, but you never seem to meet truly feminine women these days. You're a delightful change.'

She laughed. 'I have to confess, I like achieving very much, Mr Anderson. I may turn out to be the hardest-nosed harridan you've ever met!'

'Not with that face.' His eyes were luminous. 'Your soul lives in that face, Chris. Sweet, gentle, humorous; deeply and irrevocably feminine!'

'Well!' she said, secretly delighted at the over-the-top compliment. 'I'm sure you're very kind to say so, but——'

His bark of laughter interrupted her. 'You wouldn't be used to people saying things like that to you, I suppose?'

'Not in the course of work, at any rate,' she smiled.

'You'll get used to my ways,' he assured her. 'I'm not a person who can hold my feelings back. Ever. I have to speak my mind, always, whenever the mood takes me. And I do tend to speak my mind rather frankly, I'm afraid.'

'It's an admirable trait, really,' Chris assured him. She was thinking that Duncan's antipathy towards aggressive women probably explained a great deal of his shyness with interviewers. Zara Zoffany, the heroine of *Starfire*, she remembered, had been a gentle, wide-eyed, seventeen year old. In fact, all the women in his films tended to be sweetly feminine, docile women. She steered him gently towards the interview she wanted. 'You said you loved this part of the world. You come here to relax, then?'

'Exactly. I come here, or to somewhere like this, every couple of years. My work happens to be particularly exhausting, and I need to submerge myself in tranquillity...'

Discreetly, she switched on the tape-recorder, and drew her notepad towards her. The tape was for back-up only. The real essence of the interview would lie in her verbatim shorthand notes.

He was talking volubly now, eyes bright and always on the move, evidently a person who lived on his nerves. Any fears she'd had that he would be reticent disappeared. He clearly enjoyed talking about his work, and it soon became obvious that this was the sort of interview which wouldn't need much steering from her; he was perfectly content to ask his own questions, and then answer them with sometimes unsettling frankness.

She found herself wondering whether he was really going to let her print some of the things he was telling her, when she read the final copy back to him. However, that was a stile to cross later.

Two hours and three cups of tea later, he seemed to be talked out. He had given her a fascinating résumé of the making of *Starfire*, the big news of the moment. But she had been equally interested in his next project. When she brought that up, however, he raised his hands in surrender.

'No more today,' he pleaded huskily. 'My throat's aching.' Green eyes considered her speculatively. 'It's been a most fascinating conversation, Christine. If I may say so, it's rare to meet a woman as intelligent and as sensitive as you.'

'Why—thank you,' she said, taken aback.

'If you'd like to talk about my next film,' he went on, 'we could always meet again.'

'If you've got the time,' she nodded, 'I'd certainly appreciate that.'

'I have to be in town on Thursday evening.' He cocked his head at her. 'Perhaps you'll allow me to take you to dinner then?'

'That's very kind of you,' Chris said, delightedly responding to the warmth in his eyes. 'I'd love that.'

'Good. Good.' He rose, tall and good-looking. 'You
know, Chris, when I came out to this backwater, giving
my nervous system a rest was the only thing on my mind.'
He touched her arm, guiding her to the door. 'I never
expected to have my days illuminated by someone as
lovely and intelligent as you.'

Chris was late getting back, and the rumble of the presses
greeted her as she got out of the Rolls outside the *Herald*
building. Picking up a fresh copy in the foyer, she saw
that her earlier impression had been accurate. Most of
the front page, the second page, and the centre pages
were given over to various stories about the political
crisis, and photographs of the principal protagonists in
it. But the front page said it all: under the single headline
'BABEL' was a row of six photographs—six distorted,
shouting faces, each facing a different direction.

The whole thing was far closer to the slick product of
a big Fleet Street press than that of a staid provincial
newspaper.

Reading quickly through the columns in the foyer, she
couldn't help the thrill of proud excitement that flickered
along her veins. It was a fabulous edition, dynamic,
beautifully laid-out, and exercising that addictive ability
to grab the reader's attention that was the true Nash
Canfield trademark.

She read Nash's editorial in the lift. It was easy to
distinguish his work from that of the other leader-writers.
His prose had the impact of a bullet, striking straight
to the heart of the issue without fear or deviation. 'Who
loses?' the leader ended wryly. 'Why you, of course. You,
and me, and the man next door, and all the millions of
ordinary, sensible people who continue to suffer through
this deadlock.'

She shook her head in reluctant admiration as she finished it. The man might not have an ounce of tact in all his six-foot-six frame, but he had the editorial instincts of a hunting barracuda. On days like this, it really was a privilege to work for someone like Nash.

God! Was she really starting to admire the man, after all? Half-horrified, half-amused by the possibility, she walked through the corridor to the newsroom. It had the wearily jubilant atmosphere that comes after a lot of very hard work has produced an exceptional issue.

The first person she bumped into was Timothy Miller, one of the most senior reporters on the staff, and an old friend of her father's. His had been the lead article on the front page, and she congratulated him on the work.

'Thanks, Chris,' he smiled. 'I'm about whacked, I can tell you.'

The rest of the political affairs team gathered round her as she talked to Timothy. These were the senior men, experienced, dedicated journalists who'd been with the *Herald* for years. For all their hard-bitten cynicism, Chris would always be their pet, whoever was at the helm, and whatever happened to the *Herald*.

'Sam would have been proud today,' someone said, and Chris nodded.

'Yes, I think he would,' she said seriously. 'It's a very impressive edition.'

Timothy Miller stretched his lanky arms over his head. 'But it's a long, long way from Sam's style,' he said, scratching his iron-grey hair. 'Working with Nash this past week has been a revelation to me. It's more like working for one of the big nationals than for the old *Herald*...'

He had echoed Chris's own earlier thoughts. Timothy had worked in London for several years before coming back to the *Herald*, and knew what he was talking about. His eyes met hers, and apparently mistook her thoughtfulness for hurt.

'I'm not decrying Sam, Christine,' he said gently. 'I'm just saying that Nash is a different breed. He has another kind of brilliance.'

'I know what you mean,' Chris said easily. But she was surprised. Brilliant? Timothy Miller had been one of Nash's fiercest opponents at first. Was he, too, being won over by the Canfield charisma at last?

Someone took her arm. It was Tom Shoals, tall, bearded and always smiling. 'Can I see you after the weekend, Chris, about this Ransome Street story? Bob and I have some ideas we'd like to kick around for the Wednesday section.'

'No problem. We'll have a conference before the layout goes to Nash's table on Tuesday.' She shot him a wry glance. 'It isn't all going to be too sordid, is it?'

Tom grinned wickedly. 'It'll blow your socks off,' he promised, not reassuring her in the slightest.

'We're going for a drink at the Grapes,' Timothy announced, slinging his jacket over his shoulder. Whatever he felt about Nash's new style, he was too set in his ways by now to come to work in anything other than a suit. 'Are you coming?'

'Not tonight,' she said regretfully, and watched them troop out, the day's excitement still vibrant in their voices.

She walked to Nash's office, and looked through the glass panel. He was standing at the window, hands linked behind his back apparently just staring out at the snowy landscape. His Nelson pose; she smiled to herself.

She tapped, then pushed the door open. 'I've brought the keys to your Rolls back,' she said quietly, not wanting to disturb his reverie.

He didn't look round, just asked, 'How did you get on with Anderson?'

'Like a house on fire,' she said. 'I've had a lovely afternoon. He's a fascinating personality.'

Nash turned, his face tightening so quickly she thought she'd said something wrong for a moment.

'Is that so?' he rasped. 'Well, well. I trust your article will reflect more than cosy chumminess.'

'I trust so, too,' she said, using a cold voice to mask her surprise at his reaction. 'I'll do my best, anyway.' She showed him the photograph Duncan had given her. 'He says we can use this. He's very handsome, isn't he?'

Nash handed the picture back to her without comment, but his expression was anything but warm.

Rather nervously, she asked, 'When do you want the article?'

He moved to his desk purposefully, reaching for a sheaf of papers. If the day's efforts had put a strain on him, it wasn't showing—except maybe in his bad mood. 'Can you show me something by Thursday?' he asked, not looking up at her.

'If you give me till Friday,' she suggested, 'I'll have more to work with. I'm seeing him again on Thursday night.'

'What for?' he asked sharply, eyes lifting to impale her.

'There was just so much to talk about.' Realising that her tone was almost apologetic, she brought herself up shortly. Don't cringe to him, Yardley. 'Can you give me till then?' she asked, keeping it natural.

'I don't see why one interview shouldn't be quite sufficient,' he said grimly, still watching her. 'He's no genius.'

'He's a very brilliant artist,' she said, surprised again, and starting to get a little annoyed. 'I want to do him justice, Nash.'

A grim scowl crossed his passionate mouth. 'I don't pay you to produce great literature. Time is money, Yardley; did your father never teach you that?'

'I could do a much better article if you gave me the time,' she said stiffly. 'That's all.'

'What the hell!' he said with insulting bad humour. 'If you insist, you can have until Friday. After which I have plenty more for you to chew on—so get the Anderson article out of the way.'

It was an effort to keep her voice gracious. 'Thank you. I'll get it finished as soon as I can.' Trying to recover her recent feelings of warmth towards him, which had just now cooled rapidly, Chris lifted her edition of the *Herald* slightly. 'This is an absolutely stunning edition, Nash. I think it's the most exciting *Herald* I've ever seen.'

He stared at her hard for a long moment, so hard that she almost began to suspect she'd said something even more offensive to him. But the sudden smile that lit his dark eyes was like the sun coming out from storm-clouds. It seemed to warm the whole room, making her catch her breath at the sheer magnetism of the man.

'Coming from you,' he said softly, 'that's some compliment.'

'I may be prejudiced,' she replied, 'but I'm not blind to real quality.' She had meant it to sound light-hearted, but somehow it had come out husky and emotional.

The hostility between them was very quickly becoming something quite different. And suddenly she was thinking of that touch on her lips this morning. Of the fact that this was judged one of the most attractive men around. Suddenly, she was thinking of many things.

Nash's eyes narrowed to smoky bars, and for a swimming moment she almost felt he was going to step across the short space between them, and take her in his arms.

Except that the door opened at that point to admit Anita Klaus.

Anita's slanty brown eyes flicked from one to the other. 'Sorry, Nash. Didn't know you were busy. Hello, Chris,' she added with a sweetness that didn't ring very sincere. 'Aren't you frozen in that outfit?'

'I'm fine,' Chris said coolly.

Anita bared her very white teeth, her artfully tumbled mane of tawny hair giving her a carnivorous, leonine look. 'I can come back later,' she said to Nash, not moving.

'That's all right,' Nash invited. 'What did you want to see me about?'

With another Chinese-sauce glance at Chris—very sweet and sour—Anita spread some papers on the desk in front of him. 'We're having rather an argument with one of our clients,' she said, and launched into the complex advertising issue.

Anita Klaus was one person to whom Chris Yardley was definitely not a pet. And never had been. Three or four years older than Chris, she'd always made it quite clear that Chris was nothing special in her eyes, no matter who her father was. Even during Sam Yardley's time, she had always expected Chris to knuckle under whenever their paths crossed in the line of work. Fortunately, that was very seldom.

And she was very pretty. Watching her standing next to Nash's potent figure was enough to send green demons of jealousy clawing along Chris's nerveways.

'I'm afraid you're going to have to re-draft the whole thing tonight,' Nash said, sounding a damned sight more sympathetic to Anita than he ever was to Chris. 'It's a pity, but there's no way round it.'

Anita gave Nash a bright, direct smile. 'Nothing I can't handle.' She was standing unnecessarily close beside him, looking over his shoulder at the papers. 'I'll get it done,' she assured him.

Chris was tugging at the silk scarf round her slender neck, a sure sign of rising temper. Nash never apologised to *her* when heaping the work on to her plate! How well they went together, Nash's power and Anita's lithe sexiness. Damn! She couldn't get the image of them kissing out of her mind, and it burned there like a coal on tender skin.

Was Anita already Nash's lover? Did they spend the nights together, locked in passion? Maybe her presence here was interrupting a torrid scene between Nash and Anita. Like what had happened the other night. Oh, *damn* . . .

'Well, I'd better be toddling along,' Chris said tightly, suddenly very keen to get out of this orchid-house atmosphere.

Nash sent her a commanding glance. 'Wait a moment.' He leaned over his desk, sorting through the papers, a powerfully male figure completely at home in the ultra-modern setting of his office.

Gritting her teeth, Chris sat the remainder of the conversation out. The way Anita's arm kept brushing

Nash's, as though by accident, infuriated her. Why didn't Nash move away when she pressed against him?

And her blood-pressure went up another ten notches when Anita, departing, said sweetly to Nash, 'You haven't forgotten our squash date on Saturday, Nash?'

'No,' he confirmed, 'I'm looking forward to it.' And his mouth creased in one of those room-warming smiles, directed exclusively at Anita. Who sent Chris a look of sheer malice, nodded briskly, and left.

Chris was seething as she waited impatiently to see what Nash wanted of her. Unexpectedly, he lifted two crystal glasses out of a drawer, and a bottle of Bushmills. 'It's been a long, hard cold day,' he said, pouring a shot of the amber liquid into each of the glasses. 'Here.'

She took the heavy glass reluctantly. 'Is this whisky?' she asked.

Contempt at her ignorance lifted an eyebrow. 'It's a twenty-year-old single malt,' he informed her. *'Santé.'*

At least this was intimacy not offered Anita. She drank. It was fiercely strong, but also smokily mellow, and she felt it burn all the way down to her stomach. She tried not to cough. This was the sort of whisky her father had loved, and she knew enough not to ask for water to mix with it. Nash watched approvingly as she drained the glass, feeling the warmth spread through her veins. 'What did you want me for?' she asked hoarsely, setting the glass down.

'Just to give you a lift home,' he said innocently, scooping up some papers and sliding them into his leather briefcase. 'It's dark and snowing, and your car's not working.'

'I could quite easily have caught the bus,' she said stiffly, and breathed whisky-fumes.

'I haven't caught a bus in fifteen years,' Nash smiled, and shrugged on what was clearly a very expensive sheepskin coat. He looped a scarf round his neck, suddenly looking devastatingly male. 'Let's go.'

'I think I'd rather catch the bus, after all,' she decided, hating his superior air.

'Make a little sacrifice, for my sake. It'll do you good,' he said, the laconic delivery belied by the glint in his eyes. 'When you start climbing the corporate ladder, you'll travel everywhere in a white Bentley, swilling Bushmills by the bottle.'

The humour didn't ease the rankling hurt Anita had left in her. 'I still think——'

He took her arm in strong fingers. 'There are a damn sight too many chiefs round here,' he said silkily, 'and not enough indians. Let's go.'

As they walked into the foyer, Nash glanced at her set expression. 'There doesn't seem to be much love lost between you and Miss Claws,' he suggested mildly.

'We never got on,' Chris said shortly, 'even before——'

'Before what?' he asked as her sentence ground to a sudden halt.

'We just never got on. But she's a very good saleswoman.'

'Oh, that superior air,' Nash smiled, noting her slight emphasis on the last word. 'When are you going to shed all those old-fashioned literary notions, and start getting some respect for the money-making side of running a newspaper?'

'I'm learning,' she said shortly. The whisky was swimming along her veins, making her a little light-headed. 'And I can see that you appreciate Anita's— qualities.'

'Oh, I do,' Nash commented smoothly. 'She's a real asset to the paper, and she's not exactly hard to look at, either.' He shot her a wicked glance. 'Of course, she doesn't have your finesse.'

'You mean I'm insipid next to her?' Chris challenged with a stab of bitterness.

He grinned at her like a tiger contemplating its breakfast. 'You said that, Yardley, not me. Is it still snowing?'

It was indeed still snowing, so hard that the towering spire of the cathedral was barely visible through the veils of dancing flakes. Even the pavements were virginal, the day's footsteps having already been filled by fresh, clean snow.

It was bitterly cold, but the Rolls was still warm inside.

'So tell me about Duncan Anderson,' Nash invited as he drove out of the parking bay. 'What made him so marvellous?'

'Oh…' She leaned back. 'He's very sensitive. An artist to his fingertips. You sense that at once, as soon as he starts talking. He's very much…' She searched for the words. '…very much in touch with himself.'

'In touch with himself, eh?' Nash grunted. 'I've heard him described as vain and selfish.'

'That's silly,' she laughed. 'Someone who knew nothing about art or artists might say that. When you talk to him, you realise just how different he is from the ordinary man.'

'How, different?'

'He has vision,' she said dreamily. 'He has a kind of intuitive sympathy with things—almost an animal quality, though he's the most civilised man I think I've ever met.'

'Really,' Nash said quietly.

'And yet he's a paradox,' she went on, warming to the description, anticipating some of the things she would say in her article. 'Because although his medium is so highly technological, Duncan himself is a true humanist. He's a remarkable person.'

'Thank you,' Nash said drily. 'I think I get the picture, now.' The heavy car slithered in the fresh snow, and he cursed under his breath as he corrected the skid. 'I take it the admiration was mutual?' he went on grimly.

'Yes, I think he liked me.' Thinking of Anita, Chris shot Nash a look of quiet triumph. 'I know he liked me. I understood him. He told me that was rare.'

She thought she saw an expression of sheer anger cross his face for a moment, but she couldn't be certain. 'Ever heard the fable about the big fish in the little pond?' he asked smoothly.

'You think I'm too impressed by Duncan?'

'You've led a very sheltered life,' he said obliquely. 'After all, *Duncan*,' he mimicked her familiar use of his first name, 'is the first film director you've ever met.'

'*Starfire* was one of the very best films of the year,' she bridled. 'He's an international success!'

'Yeah.' He pulled the Rolls up outside her house, and turned to her. 'Just get the article written,' he said forcefully, 'and then forget him.'

'I'll certainly get the article done,' she retorted in offence. 'But if he offers me his friendship, then I'll be very honoured to take it up!'

'You might also be very unwise,' he said grimly.

'That's my problem,' she said, trying to sound supremely indifferent. But she was hurt and puzzled by his antagonism towards Duncan—after all, he hadn't even met the man. 'In any case, Nash, it has nothing whatsoever to do with you.'

His eyes glittered. 'Hasn't it?' he asked in a dangerous tone. And before she'd realised what he was doing, he had pulled her towards him, and was kissing her mouth, hard.

For a shocking moment, Chris was conscious of firm, warm male lips, of the smell of his leather coat, and the smoky tang of whisky; then she pulled away from him sharply, her heart in her throat.

'Don't!' she cried, her voice unnaturally loud in the confined space of the car.

He studied her with half-smiling eyes. 'Was that so terrible?'

'Don't you dare,' she snapped, afraid he would do it again. Her cheeks were flaming now. 'Anita Klaus may put up with this kind of thing, but I certainly won't!'

Nash leaned against the seat, watching her with an odd expression on his rugged face. 'It was only a kiss, Christine.'

'Well, it's always either a kiss or a kick, isn't it?' she said blindly, turning away and facing the snow that drifted against the window-pane.

'What does that mean?' She flinched painfully as his hands took her shoulders, drawing her gently round to face him. 'I think you'd better explain,' he said quietly, his mouth disturbingly close to hers.

'Do I have to?' She was shivering, the contact touching some raw place inside her. 'You don't have an ounce of respect for me. Editorial Consultant? What a joke! I don't know why you asked me to stay on, unless it was out of pity! I'm about as much use as a square peg in a round hole. I don't know why I don't just resign!'

'There's no question of your resigning,' he said harshly, his forcefulness putting an abrupt stop to her slipping emotions. His normally full, passionate mouth was a hard line. 'I'll ignore what you've just said as the ranting of a silly girl. I don't lavish praise on anyone. As a matter of fact, you've done well, Christine. Better than I expected, even.' He touched her arm. 'I think a lot of you——' With an effort, he stopped himself. 'Of your work. You've matured a great deal in these last months. I think you've got a real contribution to make to this newspaper—and when you've matured enough, perhaps you'll start making it.'

She flinched at the impact of his words. He went on, more gently, 'I know you feel ambivalent about the job but, believe me, your appointment isn't a Toytown one. I value you.'

He reached across her, and opened her door for her. 'Now you'd better get inside,' he commanded, 'and try to relax.'

Utterly miserable, she obeyed, closing the car door behind her. He drove off into the snowy night, the tail-lights of the Rolls-Royce gleaming like rubies.

She stared after him with swimming eyes, then went into the cold, empty house. That swiftly drunk whisky had undone a lot of things tonight, including her self-control. What had possessed her to behave like a such a damned fool? And just when things were going relatively well, too. She'd never be able to look Nash in the eyes again without blushing crimson.

Yet he'd also said things that were going to stay with her a long, long time. That he valued her. That she had a part to play in the *Herald*'s future. And maybe it had been worth the pain of that little interview, and the tears she was fighting back now, to hear those things.

# CHAPTER FOUR

DINNER with Duncan Anderson was every bit as stimulating as Chris had anticipated. The food was excellent, and the conversation ranged across a multitude of topics, from the state of the British cinema to the state of the modern marriage. Duncan's views on everything were refreshingly different. 'Marriage is an outmoded convention,' he told her over the pudding, 'which has no place in modern society.'

Chris laughed. 'You mean that?'

'It's slavery for both parties,' Duncan said seriously, running his fingers through his mane of hair. 'Why limit yourself to one partner for the rest of your life? Chris, I don't place a high value on fidelity, sexual or emotional. That's a recipe for boredom, and then stagnation. The important thing, as I tried to show in *Starfire*, is to experiment, experience, progress——'

Chris listened in silence. It was the first time in her life that she'd heard anyone talk like this, and it was both exciting and alarming. Maybe Nash was right—maybe she was a provincial little creature, brought up to honour all sorts of outmoded conventions.

'It's wonderful to talk to someone who understands,' Duncan said warmly, covering her hand with his own. 'I really do want to see more of you, Christine. A lot more of you.'

Her heart had jumped at the contact. It was disconcerting to have Duncan's vivid eyes fixed on her quite so intently. 'Well,' she smiled, letting him stroke her hand with long fingers, 'that rather depends on how long you choose to stay at the farmhouse, doesn't it?'

'Ah, the farmhouse. It's so beautiful up there,' he said, with a sigh. 'You must come up there again, little one. The woods are so dark and mysterious in winter! We can walk through them together, and smell the snow on the air...'

'You make it sound wonderful,' she agreed, gently withdrawing her hand. 'But I'm going to be frantically busy over this coming week. My boss has all sorts of tasks planned for me.'

'We'll make it this weekend, then,' Duncan decided, his handsome face brooding. 'Why not come up for Saturday and Sunday? There's plenty of room. And it's high time we got to know each other a lot better.'

The look in his eyes left her in absolutely no doubt as to what he was talking about. 'That's very kind,' she said, distinctly nervous now. 'But I'm afraid I'm going to have to work right through the weekend——'

'Nonsense!'

'I'm serious,' she smiled. 'My plate's absolutely loaded.'

'Damn,' he said softly, sitting back. 'When will I see you, then?'

'I'll try and make time next week,' she promised. He intrigued her, and she did want to see him again, but she had to be diplomatic. 'But about staying for the weekend—I don't think I could do that, Duncan. I'm afraid it wouldn't be right.'

'"*It wouldn't be right*",' he snorted. 'You sound just like my wife.'

'Are you married?' Chris asked in real, and distinctly unpleasant, surprise.

'Was,' he grimaced. '*Was* married. Oh, yes, I've made my mistake. I was married for six years, but we've been separated almost as long ago now.'

'Oh!' The information was curiously unsettling, and she stared at him wonderingly for a moment.

He smiled a trifle drily. 'It was six years of prison, Chris. She stifled me, crushed my imagination. As a person, she's a mass of insecurities and inadequacies. It was six years of hell.'

'I'm sorry to hear that,' Chris suggested, feeling a pang of compassion for Duncan.

'Her Scots Calvinist upbringing had a great deal to do with it,' he said, dismissing what was evidently a painful topic. 'Let's forget her tonight, though.'

The meal was over now, the last coffee drunk and the bill ready. He paid it with American Express, and they put on their coats in the restaurant foyer.

'I'm going to write up the interview tomorrow,' she told him, as they went out to find cabs. 'I'll probably ring you about it on Tuesday.'

'I'm very excited about it,' he said, and seemed to mean it. 'You really seem to understand me, Chris. I know it'll be a fine piece of journalism. Shall we share a cab?'

'Unfortunately, my place and yours are in opposite directions.' She smiled.

'Then we'll arrange to see each other again when you ring me on Tuesday.' He leaned forward and kissed her mouth. His lips were warm, hers cool, and she withdrew just before it could turn into anything more sensual. Stimulating as she found him, she wasn't quite won over yet. He stared down at her warmly, green eyes misty. 'Little Christine,' he murmured, 'you're something special. You know that? Something very special.'

Her head was swimming as they walked out into the snow, but whether that was Duncan, or just walking out of the hot restaurant into the icy air, she had no way of telling.

On Friday afternoon, while she was halfway through writing up the interview, a summons came in the form of a telephone call from Shrewsbury.

'Christine? How are you, dear?'

'Hello, Mum! How are *you*?'

'Both well. Charles and I want you to come up for the weekend.'

'Lovely.' She tried to make it sound bright. She had planned to work right through the weekend, as she'd told Duncan; but it had, after all, been three months since she had seen her mother and stepfather. 'Of course I'll come—but do you mind if I bring some work up with me?'

'If you insist. You'll drive up?'

'I might get the train. Dad's car—my car has been a little dodgy lately.'

'All right, dear.'

'Give Charles my love.'

'Will do. See you on Saturday. Goodbye, dear.'

'Who are you dispensing your love to?' Nash asked from the doorway of her office, making her jump.

'I didn't see you there,' she said with a nervous smile. 'Only my mother.'

'Ah.' He prowled into her office. 'I was wondering. Going down to Shropshire this weekend?'

'Mm,' she confirmed.

He studied her from the towering height of his six foot six. 'Looking forward to it?'

'Of course.' Chris gave a little shrug. 'I enjoy seeing them both.' But she couldn't keep the note of sadness out of her voice. 'I don't really see a great deal of them, as it happens.' She tilted her head, giving Nash an appealing smile. 'Families can be sad, can't they?'

'Yes.' He stared down at her for a moment. His face, normally as arrogant as any king's, had gentled. She almost felt he was going to reach out to her. 'Yes, they can.' Then, unaccountably, his expression hardened. 'But self-pity doesn't get you anywhere, Yardley. It's a luxury no one can afford. How was your night out with Anderson?'

'Super,' she said cheerfully. This was more small-talk than she'd got out of Nash in weeks, and she was quite warmed by his interest. 'We had a superb meal, and the conversation was very stimulating.'

'Lucky little you,' he said savagely. The *bonhomie* had disappeared like water in a desert. 'At what stage of the evening did he try to kiss you?'

'That's an unwarranted implication,' she flushed, responding instantly to his inexplicable change of mood. 'I'm honoured that a man like Duncan wants my friendship—and friendship's all he wants!'

'In my experience,' he said drily, 'friendship is not the main thing middle-aged men want from a pretty young girl.'

'It's not like that,' she snapped. 'Duncan is different!'

He shrugged, hard-eyed. '*Plus ça change . . .* It's your business. Just get that interview written.' He dropped something on her desk. 'Then you can get busy with this.'

She picked it up. It was a simple list of names, and she recognised most of them as the town's leading legal, artistic and financial people. There was also a sprinkling of Hons, Sirs and Ladies, and one Rt Honourable. 'What is this?' she asked.

'It's an invitation list. I've been editor of the *Herald* for over six months now, and I haven't thrown a dinner-party in this town yet. I'm going to remedy that in two weeks' time. And I need you to be there.'

'Funny,' she said warily, looking up at him, 'that doesn't sound like an invitation.'

'Don't you want to come?' he enquired smoothly. 'It'll be the social event of the year.'

'Of course! I do hope these yokels come up to your sophisticated anticipation,' she said acidly, but reflected that he was probably right. Nash Canfield's first dinner-party in this town would definitely rate high on the social calendar.

'That's why I want you there.' There was a glint in his eye which ought to have warned her. 'I shall want you to hold my hand while I meet the local dignitaries.'

'And show that the last of the Yardleys approves of the *Herald*'s new editor?' she guessed drily.

'Naturally,' he replied, inclining his head. 'You're so keen on tradition—now's your chance to show that the tradition is carrying on. And I want your help in arranging the evening.'

'My help?'

He sat on the desk, looming over her. 'Didn't you help your father throw parties like this one?'

'Yes, but——'

'A bachelor on his own doesn't make as good a host as a man and woman together,' he informed her flatly. 'I need you. Catering by Wenham's, flowers from Osprey's, hospitality by Canfield and Yardley.' He gave her that tiger's grin. 'Sounds good, doesn't it?'

'No, it doesn't,' she contradicted, taken aback. 'Aren't there any other women in your life?' She crossed her long legs with a rustle of silk, and with a flash of sheer malice, suggested, 'What about Anita?'

'I never combine business with pleasure,' he said, a mocking huskiness in the deep voice. 'This party will be strictly business.'

'Indeed?' Chris snapped, anger flowering inside her. If he'd had any chance of getting her to co-operate, he'd just blown it! 'Well, I'm going to be busy all next week, so you'll have to ask Anita after all. And now, I'm busy!' She swung her chair on its castors and turned her back on him stiffly. Without effort, Nash took hold of the chair-back and swung her right round to face him.

'Hello again,' he said calmly, dark eyes compelling her to listen. 'I hadn't finished yet. Your presence is important, Chris. Not just because you're Sam Yardley's daughter, either—because of that special touch you've got. You'll make all the difference.'

She stared up at him rebelliously. Why couldn't he just say he wanted her there for her own sake? The tiniest hint of warmth in his invitation, and her whole attitude would have been transformed. 'I see,' she said flatly.

'I've already taken care of the invitations,' he informed her. 'In the meantime, pay a visit to Osprey's to decide on the flowers, and to Wenham's to sort out the meal. They'll be expecting you—and there's no budget. Also—you know these people; I don't. I want you to organise the seating the way you think best, with the right people facing each other. Not to mention the lighting, and so forth. That means a visit to my apartment to check everything out. Better make that Monday night.' He hesitated for the first time. 'Please?'

Chris stared at him, her mouth a mutinous line. 'What if I refuse?' she suggested tightly.

He still had a hold on the back of her chair, and now he pulled her forward so that she had to tilt her head to look up into his face from about a foot away.

'What if you obey—for once in your disobedient little life?'

'You're a dictator,' she said helplessly, almost hypnotised by his closeness. His skin was surprisingly fine. That deep-chiselled mouth had a velvety texture, an irresistible authority... 'Did you say Wenham's?' she asked, naming the best restaurant in town.

'Yes,' he nodded. 'I did say Wenham's.'

'What sort of food were you thinking of?' she asked, looking at him with beautiful amethyst eyes.

'You choose,' he invited. 'Something positive, something with a theme. It's up to you.'

She sighed. 'I suppose they do game very well...' Chris rose, and went to get her Yellow Pages. Black eyes flickered to her legs as she walked across the office.

'Jeans?' he enquired drily, glancing at her legs.

'Your idea,' she reminded him with a grin. 'You told me I looked ravishing in jeans. Besides, they are designer jeans,' she pointed out, and turned cheekily to show him the expensive label on her neatly hugged bottom.

He came to her, fluid as a panther, his eyes glittering so hungrily that for a bone-melting moment she thought he was going to crush her in his arms. But he stopped short, leaving her lungs suddenly oxygenless, and merely took her elbow in steel fingers, turning her so that he could study the silk blouse that clung to the curve of her breasts, the sheer line of the denims, and the soft suede boots she had tucked them into.

'Don't you approve?' she asked, trying to sound flippant, but coming out merely husky.

'Not exactly,' he said, his deep voice a menacing rumble as he released her.

'Is it really unsuitable?' Chris asked anxiously, pulling her shining-clean hair away from her face.

'No. But I'm selfish enough to want to be the only man who sees you in jeans.' The softly growled words sent an odd ripple down her back. 'How long has it been since you attended a party, Yardley?'

'I'm always going to parties,' she said, slightly defensive at the unexpected question.

'Plenty of men in your life, eh?'

'Plenty,' she assured him, irritated to death by that mocking smile. 'All I want, at any rate!'

'Hmmm.' He contemplated the perfect red leaf of her mouth, as though wondering how many male lips it had kissed. 'Well, if there's anyone from among the glittering throng of your friends that you feel like inviting, feel free...'

'Anyone?' she echoed.

'Of course.'

'Then,' she said with a glitter of inspiration, 'I'm going to ask Duncan Anderson.'

'*Minx.*' She was alarmed at the flare of real anger that ripped across his eyes, but it was almost instantly hooded, like a furnace being banked down. His fingers bit into her arms painfully, then relaxed, releasing her. She was almost regretting that little piece of provocation, now, but it had been worth it to annoy him to this extent. His voice deepened threateningly. 'I don't want Duncan Anderson at my party.'

'No Duncan,' she said firmly, 'no Christine.'

'I don't like the man——'

'You don't know him. You'll enjoy meeting Duncan,' she said sweetly. That would teach him, at any rate, not to be quite so imperious with her in future!

'You're just doing this to annoy me,' he accused grimly.

'Certainly not,' she snorted. 'I like Duncan very much. And as it happens, he'll mix very well with all your guests. So if he can't come, then I'm not coming either.'

She watched his broad shoulders as he walked out of her office without another word. It was the first time, to her knowledge, that anyone had scored over Nash Canfield. Amusement struggled with regret in her. She'd enjoyed winning an argument very much for a change. What hadn't been so funny was the look on his face as he had walked out.

She sat down, her legs slightly shaky, and studied the list. She had been deliberately lying about her social life to Nash. As it happened ...

As it happened, she thought wryly, being editor of the Wednesday Review had brought her into contact with more people than she knew how to deal with. And yet her love-life had been utterly barren since Nash had arrived.

Why? Was it grief over her father's death? Was it something to do with Nash himself? Maybe the very fact that he kept her in a perpetual state of irritation had obsessed her. Certainly, in the past six months she had only been out with men a handful of times.

Since her parents' divorce, she had been keeping men at arm's length anyway. No special reason. No traumas or anything. Just a certain—disillusionment. The precious dreams she had once explored had been hidden away, deep inside her, and she no longer cared to even remember that she'd once dreamed them.

In fact, she realised with a faint, wry smile, the only real man in her life these days was Nash Canfield.

She found herself staring at the painting on her wall. That starburst of light was so vivid, so powerful. Like Nash, it was almost too full of life to be easily handled.

Like Nash, it had something larger than life. Power. And maybe beauty.

'How are you finding working for Nash Canfield?' her mother asked on Sunday afternoon, absently adjusting Chris's bright, fair hair as they sat in the heated conservatory having tea.

'Challenging,' Chris smiled. 'He's producing a very different paper from Dad's *Herald*.'

'Yes,' Lucille agreed drily. 'He's making it pay. Clever man. It must be very satisfying to work for him.'

'He makes rather formidable demands on me,' Chris sighed.

'Ah. That's a sign he respects you. I take it you get on with him?'

'In a work context, yes.'

'And out of work?'

'Actually, it's hard to say *what* I feel about him,' Chris admitted with sad candour. 'He's just——' She shrugged, at a loss for easy words to describe Nash. 'Just so abrasive. As though he's been fighting for so long that he's forgotten he's already won the battle.'

Her stepfather grunted from behind his *Observer*. 'The man's got a long way to go yet. The rumour is that he's on the look-out for another newspaper.'

'That's the first I've heard,' Chris shrugged. 'But it's not impossible.'

'Is he handsome?' her mother asked.

'Very,' Chris nodded. Oddly, it occurred to her that she would have given a very different answer a few weeks ago. It had taken her a long, long time to realise that Nash was one of the most beautiful men she had ever set eyes on.

Her mother studied her thoughtfully. 'Pots of money, I suppose?'

'Pots.' Chris smiled wryly. Money had always been vitally important to her mother. She had divorced Chris's father for the unforgivable sin of putting all of his into the *Herald*; and Chris sometimes felt sure that she'd married the frankly stuffy and boring Charles Crocker mainly because he had plenty more.

'Hmm.' Lucille studied the blazing diamond ring on her delicate left hand, her face still lovely in early middle age. 'It's not totally out of the question.'

'What isn't totally out of the question?' Chris asked curiously.

Lucille smiled a secret smile. 'A ride. It seems to have stopped raining. Charles, is it too wet for Christine to take one of the horses out?'

Monday morning was invariably the busiest part of the week. Besides the fact that she was busy with the middle passages of the Duncan Anderson interview, the weekend had also turned up a mass of copy connected with the Ransome Street story.

The police were struggling to stop the influx of low-life characters from Manchester, but the problem was notoriously hard to take positive action against. In the meantime, house-prices had plummeted in the area. At least six decent families had sold up and cleared out this year alone, and into their places, taking advantage of the low prices, was moving a tide of big-city undesirables. Even more dismaying, problems more serious than prostitution were now being hinted at.

In a telephone conversation with one of her contacts in the local police, Chris got an off-the-record account of a sharp rise in drug dealing and addiction in the area. Nash had been right; the problem was a deadly serious one. Her face was creased with worry as she put the phone down.

'Not exactly what Daddy's little girl is used to, is it?'

Chris looked up to see Anita Klaus leaning against her doorway, smiling at her without humour. 'Did I hear you mention addicts? And prostitutes?' she went on. 'Getting your dainty little fingers dirty, I see. I wish you could see your face, Chris. You look like a princess who's found something nasty on her shoe.'

She came all the way in, closing the door behind her, and Chris looked up at her warily. Wearing a tight dress in the flame-red she favoured, Anita was obviously more than usually combative this morning. No doubt she would soon find out why.

'It's going to be a fascinating story,' she said carefully.

'Don't give me that,' Anita snorted. 'You loathe every minute of it.'

'What can I do for you, Anita?' Chris asked, side-stepping the whole issue, which in any case had nothing whatsoever to do with the advertising section.

'A little information,' Anita said smoothly. 'Is it true that you're playing hostess at Nash's apartment in a fortnight's time?'

Chris felt her nerves tightening in response to Anita's question. So that was it. 'Nash asked me to help out, yes.'

'Well, well.' Folding her arms round a folder, Anita leaned against the door, her eye slitted. 'You are going for the jugular, aren't you? Driving Nash's Rolls. Organising his dinner-parties. What next?'

'Nothing next.'

'Oh, come!' Anita's bright-red dress reflected angry lights in her eyes. 'Do you take me for an idiot? I've seen the way you look at him. As though he were the only man in the world. Do you really think it's such a damned secret?'

Suddenly breathless, Chris could only shake her head. 'You've got the wrong idea, Anita.'

Anita laughed shortly. 'No, I haven't. You're trying your damnedest to become a proper little editor's pet!' Contempt curved her mouth. 'You think Nash respects you because of who your father was?'

'I'm perfectly aware of Nash's feelings about my father's style of editorship,' she said stiffly.

'That's right,' Anita agreed, nodding her tawny crop of hair significantly. 'Because your father was running this paper into the ground. If it hadn't been for that heart attack, there wouldn't even be a *Herald* right now, would there?'

'And if it wasn't for my father giving you a job in the first place,' Chris said sharply, 'you wouldn't be here right now either—would you, Anita?'

'I'm worth twice what Nash pays me,' Anita spat. 'Which is more than can be said for you!' She covered her flash of real anger with a false smile. 'Poor little Chris,' she said ironically. 'You dream about him at nights, don't you? Are you really as crazy about him as you make out? Or are you a lot cleverer than I give you credit for?'

'Not that it's any of your business,' Chris said fiercely, 'but I don't have any designs on Nash whatsoever. Why are you so keen to believe otherwise?'

'Because I'm not blind to the way you've wormed yourself into Nash's confidence,' came the grim reply. 'You're trying to get between him and me!'

'Oh? Are you having trouble getting access to the editor?' Chris asked innocently.

'Don't play with me!' Anita slammed her hand down on Chris's desk, an oddly masculine gesture. 'You were Queen Bee around here when your father was alive,' she snarled. 'Everybody's pretty little pet! But since he died, you've been cut down to size, and you can't handle that, can you? So you've decided to get your hooks into Nash!'

'Oh, for God's sake,' Chris said impatiently. 'I haven't got the time for this, Anita. If things are going badly between you and Nash, I can assure you it's got nothing to do with me!'

'Who told you things were going badly between me and Nash?' Anita demanded in a tight voice.

'Why else are you here?' Chris shrugged. She rose, slim and compact, and walked past Anita to her door. 'This really isn't newspaper business, and in any case, it's too childish to bother with. Can we terminate the conversation?'

'Childish, is it?' Anita faced her dangerously. 'You're not at your exclusive public school now, Chris. It isn't all jolly girls together any more. You start coming between me and Nash and you'll regret it! Stick to Duncan Anderson—he's more your type!'

'Right,' Chris snapped, her eyes darkening to slate-grey as her temper gave way. 'Shall we take this little problem to the editor right now, then? I really think you should have the chance to put your complaints to him in person!'

Anita stared hotly into Chris's eyes for a long moment. Then she shook her mane of leonine hair. 'I don't think you've got the guts for the fight I'll give you.' She bared those sharp white teeth in a humourless smile. 'And you haven't got enough about you to keep a man like Nash.'

Chris just pulled the door open silently, too angry to bandy words any longer. With a sneer, Anita walked swiftly out.

Feeling shaken to the core, Chris went back to her desk and sat down. Anita's words had stripped a whole layer of tender skin off her mind, leaving a raw place. Did she really look at Nash in that way? Was she really under some kind of spell?

The telephone buzzed insistently into her whirling thoughts, and she picked it up numbly.

'Yardley?' Nash's growl didn't lose any of its force over the telephone. 'Care to have lunch with me?'

'I'm busy,' she snapped, feeling that Nash was the last person she wanted to see.

'Don't be silly,' he replied calmly. 'No one's too busy to lunch with me. I've booked a table at the St George's Grill Room. Come to my office in ten minutes.' The line clicked dead in her ear.

Under a spell? She pulled on her coat tensely, reflecting that one of the things she felt most strongly about Nash was the way he controlled her. He exerted a kind of power over her which was both deeply appealing, and yet also frightening. She wasn't used to giving anyone that degree of control over her life.

Anita's vicious attack had disturbed her deeply. How much truth had there been in what she'd said? *Was* Nash having an affair with Anita Klaus?

It was all too horribly possible. And the thought sent a nauseating pain through her heart. Did she really care so much about him, then? And if they *were* having an affair, then where did Chris herself stand? Piggy in the middle? A bit on the side for Nash? An irrelevant bystander?

If there were answers to those questions in her heart, Chris couldn't find them now. The only thing she did know was that she knew next to nothing about Nash Canfield.

The grill room was one of the smartest places in town, and very crowded.

'Don't you ever get sick of the good life?' she asked him wryly as they settled down at their table. 'I mean, after the kind of childhood you had, the lifestyle you've got now must seem just a little unreal.'

'It does, sometimes,' he admitted. 'But a long time ago, my dear Chris, I made a simple decision—that life was too short to accept anything less than the best. All the time. It's not just a question of enjoying the good life, as you call it. It's simply a way of living—doing your best, expecting the best in return.'

'I bow my head to your superior knowledge of life,' Chris said with a slight smile.

'How was your weekend?' he asked.

'Better than usual,' she admitted. 'Sometimes I can feel quite close to my mother.'

He watched her face. 'I've often wondered . . . why did your parents get divorced?'

She shrugged awkwardly, the ground still too sensitive to be trodden on lightly. 'It had a lot to do with the *Herald*'s failing finances. My father had to prop it up with his own money, and it took just about everything he had. My mother thought he was mad.' Chris glanced at Nash obliquely. 'She couldn't understand his love for the *Herald*. She thought she should come first. She made him choose,' she said tersely, the memories bitter, 'and he chose the paper. So she asked for a divorce.'

'I don't have to ask whether you suffered,' he said quietly. 'I know that you did.'

'How?' she asked in surprise.

'I've always known. The hurt is there, inside you, still.' He reached for her hand, and traced the veins with his own tanned fingers, his mouth taking on a wry smile. 'But it's all behind you now, Chris. It will fade.'

Chris just nodded, a lump in her throat. He had an insight into her feelings that went almost frighteningly deep.

Maybe Anita was halfway right, after all. Maybe she felt a lot more for Nash Canfield than she was used to admitting.

'Anyway,' she said with an effort at a smile, 'you must have been hurt far worse than I've ever been. I guess you've been put off the idea of marriage for life?'

'Not at all,' he said easily. 'I regard getting married, and having a family, as the most important ambition of my life.'

*'You?'* She stared at him. It was the very last answer she would have expected from Nash. 'You're joking!'

'Why do you say that?'

'What on earth would you want with a wife and child?' she demanded, almost laughing at the idea. 'I'd expect to see Lucifer in church first!'

'It isn't such a strange ambition,' he said quietly, looking into her eyes. 'It's one I've had for a long, long time, Chris. I was more or less abandoned as a boy. As you probably know, my mother didn't have a great deal of time for a child. She was kind to me when I saw her, but that wasn't very often. I never knew who my father was. I ran wild on the streets. I took some hard knocks on the way up the ladder. And I always swore to myself that no child of mine would ever have to struggle like that.' He grinned suddenly, illuminating the brooding darkness of his expression. 'My views on marriage are equally conservative, as you can imagine. I have not the slightest intention of indulging in a divorce, extra-marital affairs, an open marriage, or any of the other bizarre trends that are so popular these days. My ideal is a lifelong devotion to one partner, the mother of my child—and to give them both all the love I can.'

Chris simply stared at him. She'd never dreamed of hearing sentiments like these from Nash's lips. 'I'm sorry if I look a little dazed,' she said wryly. 'I just find all this a little hard to square with your Don Juan image——'

Nash interrupted with a scornful exclamation. 'That's a fantasy, Christine! Any half-way-attractive bachelor with a little money becomes the focus of gossip and fantasy. It's very tiresome, and it's one of the aspects of success that I've found most hard to deal with.'

Their food arrived. The mixed grill was delicious, served with a crisp salad and a ripe, full-bodied Chianti.

'What about you?' Nash asked with deceptive casualness as they started to eat. 'How do you feel about marriage and a family?'

'I don't have any feelings at all,' she said calmly. It wasn't true, but she was damned if she was going to open up in front of Nash Canfield. Just because he'd kissed her once or twice didn't give him the right to all her inner secrets! 'Like you, my experience of family life wasn't all that hot. So I've no intention of subjecting any poor child to the same misery.'

'You mean you don't want children?' Nash demanded, eyes narrowing to fierce slits.

'Is that so surprising in these liberated days?' she replied indifferently, and took a mouthful of wine.

'Your casualness is the surprising thing,' he said. 'When you think of all the women who want children more than anything on earth, and who can't have any for one reason or another——' He shook his head. 'Is your career that much more important?'

'Easily,' she said shortly. Damn him! He always managed to put her back up so that she ended up arguing for a position she didn't really believe in. 'I have my own life to lead. I'm not a baby-machine, nor was I born to slave over some man's dirty dishes!'

'No one's talking about making you into a baby-machine,' Nash said impatiently, forgetting to eat. 'Having children and a husband doesn't stop you from having a career. But no life—man's or woman's—can be fulfilled without loving relationships.'

'You can have those without the servitude of marriage.'

'You sound as though you're quoting,' he said suspiciously.

'I am.' She smiled serenely. 'From Duncan Anderson.'

'That idiot,' he growled.

'Duncan has his head screwed on right,' she told Nash with an infuriating coolness she was far from feeling. His passionate defence of marriage had moved her in a way she didn't even want to explore, but she wasn't going to show him *that*. 'He may not have your macho drive, but at least he's woken up to the twentieth century.'

Nash's fist crashed on to the table with enough force to make the crockery sing, and heads to turn at nearby tables. 'I will not sit here and listen to you preaching these infantile philosophies,' he rasped, eyes burning angrily into hers. 'You think you can casually dismiss something that's been the mainstay of the human race for the past fifty thousand years? Who the hell do you think you are, sneering at marriage and parenthood?'

'I wasn't sneering,' Chris said, her face paling under Nash's anger. 'I was just trying to point out that the traditional views don't necessarily hold for a modern woman with her own life to lead.'

'Well, for God's sake don't quote Duncan Anderson on the subject,' Nash growled, tackling his steak as though he were cutting an enemy's throat. 'Choose some other guru. Or, better still, develop some ideas of your own!'

Her mouth closed to a sullen line. Some ideas of her own? The cheek!

She had argued with him just for the sake of irritating him. The truth was that her feelings about marriage and having children were so precious to her, and went so deep into her heart, that she dared not expose them to Nash Canfield. If he'd had an ounce of sensitivity in his body, he would have realised that people whose parents had gone through a traumatic divorce didn't find it easy to talk about subjects like that.

And she didn't need to consult Duncan for opinions on topics as important as marriage and parenthood—she could make her own mind up, thank you very much!

The atmosphere was suddenly oddly strained after that exchange, Nash looking as though she'd really upset him. And just when they had been getting on so well, that fierce antagonism giving way to a kind of affectionate banter that had started making her feel so warm inside.

But why? she wondered unhappily. Her views didn't matter a curse to him. Or did they? He was expecting her to keep slaving over her desk at the *Herald*, not trying to marry her off to some male chauvinist sheikh in a particularly conservative Gulf state.

'Anyway,' she said, brooding over the dessert list, 'you'd blow your top if I suddenly announced I was leaving the *Herald* to marry some nice young man and raise a family of squalling brats.' She glanced up at him with impudent eyes. 'Wouldn't you?'

He glared at her darkly. 'Try it and see.'

'So the question of my getting married doesn't even arise,' she said with dignity. 'I'm going to have the *crème caramel*, please.'

'Sometimes,' Nash glowered, looking as though he almost meant it, 'you drive me crazy, Yardley. Have your *crème caramel*, and I hope it chokes you.'

'Temper,' she reproved, exulting behind her serene expression. That made the second time in three days that she had succeeded in infuriating Nash! 'Do you still want me to come over to your apartment tonight?' she asked sweetly. 'Or do you want someone less liberated to organise your dinner-party?'

'Just be in my office at five-thirty,' he said with controlled savagery, and snapped his fingers for the waiter.

# CHAPTER FIVE

BY THE end of the day, which had included several more interviews with various people, a long discussion with the news editor, and an afternoon of furious energy devoted to her keyboard, Chris's mood was much more subdued. She was weary enough to loll back in the leather seat and doze as Nash drove her across town to his apartment, which overlooked the river.

She was almost asleep when she felt his arm slide around her shoulders and draw her close to him. She tensed in panic for a second, every nerve shrilling an alarm. Then her head was pillowed on his broad chest, and it was as though every bone had melted inside her. With a helpless sigh, she let herself relax, taking comfort from Nash's warm male body and the delicious support of his arm around her. 'You look about all in,' he rumbled, touching her hair with his lips. 'Do I really give you a tough time?'

'You certainly don't seem to notice that you wear people out,' she said, her mouth against Nash's shirt-front. Comfortable this might be, but it was doing terrible things to her pulse-rate. She sat upright again, her cheeks touched with colour, and started pulling her hair into order. Inwardly she was wondering how on earth she'd been so soft as to melt into his arms like that. Like a sparrow waltzing into a fox's mouth! 'Oh, dear.' She pointed guiltily to the smudge of her red lipstick against Nash's silk shirt. 'Mine, I think.'

'Sloppy.' Dark eyes laughed into hers. 'If I had a wife, that might be difficult to explain away.' As they walked up the back stairs to the apartment, he informed her, 'I bought one of these apartments the day we agreed terms on my purchase of the *Herald*. I wanted somewhere close to the river, yet not too far from the office.'

She couldn't help gasping with pleasure as she stepped into the vast drawing-room in the penthouse suite. One whole wall had been turned into a series of sliding glass doors, giving a stunning panoramic view of the river and the countryside beyond in the moonlight. Nash slid one of the tall glass doors open for her, and she walked out on to the balcony. She leaned on the railing, watching the tranquil beauty of the ancient river that had fed this town for millenia, drinking in the peace of the evening that was settling over the world.

'It's quite staggering,' she said quietly, 'what money and taste can do.'

'You like it?' He was watching her intently.

'I love it, of course,' she said. The breeze stirred the shining sweep of her hair as she turned to him. 'It must make a hell of a change from——'

'From the world I grew up in,' he supplied gently as she hesitated. 'Yes, as a matter of fact it does.' He tugged his tie down and slipped his jacket off. 'Like your drink out here?'

'Not likely—I'm much too curious about the rest of your apartment,' she said briskly.

'Come on, then.' She walked back into the room ahead of him, silvery eyes drifting from the black hide furniture in the sunken conversation-pit to the glass case displaying a dazzling collection of china that must be worth thousands, to the eighteenth-century paintings on the silk-papered walls, to the unbelievably fine suit of *samurai* armour that stood next to a sideboard that might be—*had* to be—Chippendale, to the sensual life-size Marucci bronze of a nude woman that really ought to have been in an art gallery...

'Who did this place for you?' she asked in an awed whisper.

'I *did* it, as you so crudely put it, myself.'

'All this?' She had only just noticed that the carpets were collector's Persian, each one a jewel of shimmering colour. 'When on earth did you learn about all this stuff?'

'Do I really strike you as that savage?' he enquired drily, pouring drinks.

'I didn't mean that,' she said, flushing. 'But you deliberately project this hard, soulless image. It's rather surprising, to say the least, to come here and find a sort of earthly paradise.'

'You're too kind.' He pressed a button on the complex-looking stereo system, and Mozart slid sweetly into the room via concealed speakers. That same piano concerto, the one that made her ache with pleasure.

Chris closed her eyes and sank back into the soft embrace of a chair with her drink.

'You really are a very unpredictable man,' she said dreamily. 'Mmm, I love that music...'

'So do I.' It was infuriating to have to admit that the man she had enjoyed thinking of as a barbarian turned out to have the most superb taste—and the money to back it up.

He walked across the room, moving with the unconscious grace of a panther, and touched a switch in the panelling. A section of the wall slid smoothly back, as Chris watched in amazement, revealing a dining alcove that was just big enough to accommodate the long table and its twelve chairs. It, too, commanded the same view of the river. 'There's access to this room from the kitchen,' he informed her casually. 'I thought we'd leave the door closed until it was time to eat, by which time the Wenham's staff will have set the dinner on the table. We can eat in the intimacy of the alcove, and then come back in here afterwards.'

'Closing the door again,' Chris supplied, shaking her head, 'while invisible servants clear away the mess.'

'Exactly.'

'For a slum-kid, you've developed some very aristocratic notions,' she said.

'I do my best,' he said, leaning against the wall as he studied her elegant, light movements. She had the uncomfortable feeling that he could see right through her snug denims and boots to the creamy skin beneath.

'You have a habit of staring at me,' Chris commented, coming down the stairs from the dining-alcove and facing him with a confidence she was very far from feeling.

'I'm interested in you.'

She cradled her drink in both hands, dropping her gaze with a fluttering heart. 'In what way?'

'In a lot of ways.' He slipped an arm through hers, oblivious to her stiffness, and walked her back to the sofa. 'Take that touch-me-not expression off your face, Chris,' he commanded. 'Let's go through to the kitchen.'

That, too, was a design masterpiece. Nash was fascinated by machinery, she thought, glancing round at the sophisticated catering technology he'd had built in to the white-tiled kitchen. Planning the party was starting to take on overtones of excitement. Thoroughly wrapped up in what she was doing, she traced through every step of the evening with him. The dining-table itself was

massive enough for her to have no problems with the
seating arrangements. Nash at the head, of course——

'And you at the other end,' he said firmly. 'You'll be
the hostess, Chris.' He pointed to a concealed button at
that end of the table. 'That activates a buzzer in the
kitchen to signal that you're ready for the next course.
Personally, I'd rather people took as long as they wanted
over each course. There's no sense in rushing our guests
through the meal.'

'No,' she agreed, 'you're right.' She glanced at the
two niches that flanked the conversation-area. 'Those
are perfect for big bouquets of flowers,' she decided.
'But we'll need more room than you've got at present.
We'll put the piano out in the hallway, if you're
agreeable, and move those two Chinese screens somewhere else. Then you can let people gravitate between
three different areas.' She walked across the carpets,
musing. 'Best to steer the more elderly guests down here,
when they can sit in comfort. The younger ones will
prefer to be able to circulate, anyway. What a pity it
won't be warm enough to have the balcony open...'

He was watching her with a slow smile. 'Know what
I like about you?' he said softly. 'You always give one
hundred percent, no matter whether you like the job
you've been given or not. That's a very rare quality.'

She shrugged. 'That's the way I am, Nash. It's the
way my father brought me up.'

'And it's a quality you've had to call on a great deal
in the past six months, hmm?'

'I don't know what you mean,' she said, refusing to
be drawn.

'Oh, come,' he smiled. 'We're both off-duty now. You
can hardly tell me you've found the past half-year easy,
can you?'

'No,' she agreed slowly. 'It hasn't been easy. But then, I never expected it to be. Losing my father wasn't easy. Finding out that I had to lose the *Herald* wasn't easy, either. Some of it's been very hard.'

'You haven't lost the *Herald*, Christine.' His voice was gentle. 'It's still your paper.'

'No. It's yours.' But she smiled as she said the words. She had always been afraid of Nash Canfield. Right from the start she'd been fighting him, struggling against his iron will as though fighting for her very life. She had detested him at times, loathed his brashness and his overwhelming male self-confidence, and she'd certainly left him in no doubt as to her feelings about what he'd done to the *Herald*.

Yet in the past weeks something else had surfaced between them—a mutual regard, for want of a better phrase. And while it hadn't made Nash any easier to live with for her, it had allowed her to look beyond her prejudices, and see more of the man than ever before...

Nash grinned unexpectedly, as though he'd read her thoughts. 'Resistance is good for me. If I had a team of yes-men, I'd know that the *Herald* was really dying. Don't think your moderating influence isn't one of the reasons I want you to stay!' He walked over to her, and took her arm. 'You *do* give a hundred percent, Chris, all the time. That's why I value you more than any of the others. For them, it's just a job. To you, it's something much more.' He took her chin in his hand, turning her face so that he could stare into her eyes, hypnotic, compelling. Suddenly, the gleam of a smile illuminated those midnight-deep eyes of his. 'Do you really think of me as an enemy?'

'Well,' she flustered, 'there is a certain antagonism, you can't deny that. It tends to cloud the issue——'

'Odd. I find it stimulating rather than otherwise.' His eyes were brooding on her lips now. 'I wouldn't change it for the world.' He leaned forward, covering her unsuspecting mouth with his own.

His kiss was hard, warm, heart-stoppingly intimate. It paralysed her, only her eyes moving as they widened into dazed pools. Then panic surfaced in her, and he let her struggle away from him, breathless and scarlet-cheeked.

'This isn't a very good idea,' she gasped, her emotions swirling in chaos.

Nash laughed huskily, desire for her burning like a flame in his eyes. 'Anyone would think you'd never been kissed before.' She flinched as he stroked the silky sheen of her hair. 'I've been wanting to do that for a long, long time, Christine.' He cupped the delicate oval of her face in his hands, eyes brooding on her mouth. 'Don't look so appalled.'

Her fingers closed round his wrists shakily. 'I—I think I'd better go, Nash. Before——'

'Before you acknowledge your own feelings?' He kissed her again, almost harshly this time, his lips hungry and demanding, his fingers roaming hungrily through her scented hair. 'It isn't all hostility, is it?'

Chris was too stunned by the passion of the onslaught even to struggle, her eyes closing helplessly as his lips crushed hers, forcing them to part with ruthless purpose, his tongue thrusting between her lips, searching for the passion of her response.

Her whole body seemed to be on fire, every nerve stretched tight with an excitement that was almost fear. She should have been clawing at him to make him stop, but instead she was giving way to an eruption of feeling that seemed to have been building up inside her for weeks. The power of his body was overwhelming, a crushing force that was terribly, frighteningly sweet to surrender to. She clung to him, feeling the heat of his body, the surge of need and desire in him.

'Chris,' he whispered, his mouth roaming over her face, touching her eyes, her temples, the bruised satin of her mouth. The kissing gave way to another kind of hunger, a driving need inside her that urged her against him, forcing a whimper from her throat as his hand cupped her breast, the aroused peak thrusting into his palm through the silk of her blouse. Why wasn't she fighting him, struggling against this outrage?

'You're shaking like a leaf,' he said quietly, cradling her in his arms. It was true; she could hardly control the fingers that sought to restore some order to her tumbled hair. She had disintegrated completely under that devastatingly expert attack, all her carefully maintained poise thrown to the winds. He wouldn't let her go, holding her close as though he couldn't get enough of her. 'Did I hurt you?'

'Yes,' she whispered, touching her tender lips. 'That's what you wanted, isn't it? Please let me go.'

'In this mood?' he asked mockingly. He pulled her down on to the sofa beside him. 'I want you far too much, Miss Yardley.' Her mouth was open to protest as he kissed her; but this time he was intoxicatingly gentle, his lips teasing and caressing as softly as the touch of a moth's wing. The savage masculinity had become a tenderness that melted her bones inside her, that dissolved her resistance. Her whole being was concentrated on the warm, moist mouth against her own, the tongue that traced her lips, probing her inner sweetness, tasting her as though she'd been some exquisite flower.

Half whispering his name, she clung to him, all her antagonism towards him totally forgotten. It was so long since her senses had been filled like this, since her body had responded in this infinitely sensual way. Or had it ever responded like this? Nash was, by her own admission, the most masculine man she had ever met. Why hadn't that registered with her before? His maleness was overwhelming, a quality that had dominated her reactions to him from the start. Now it was tearing her apart, the confrontation that had been brewing so long in full flood—but that in a way she'd never anticipated!

'Chris, you know where this is leading,' he growled, the deep rumble of passion alive in his voice.

*'No!'* The vision of his magnificent body naked against hers, invading her soul, was terrifying. She pulled away. 'You're completely wrong for me, Nash!'

'Wrong?' His eyes narrowed into smoky slits as his fingers bit into her arms. 'What the hell does that mean?'

'We're opposites, can't you see that?' she said shakily. 'Like black and white!'

'With me cast as black,' he suggested with grim humour, 'and you as white. Is that it?'

'We've got nothing in common.'

'Nothing?'

'You'd destroy me.' Her voice was trembling and unsteady.

'I assure you,' he smiled, 'destroying you is the last thing on my mind.'

'I'm not ready for whatever you've got in mind!' Pulling even further away from him, she went on tensely, 'You've got into the habit of just grabbing what you want, Mr Canfield. Well, that doesn't include me! I've watched you have your way with the *Herald*, and I've got no intention of letting you do the same thing to me.'

His expression changed as though she'd slapped his face. 'By God,' he said softly, 'you run it close to the wind sometimes, Christine!'

She'd scored at last. She hardened her voice. 'I'm not one of your easy conquests, Nash. I never will be.'

'That's what makes it fun,' he said, eyes dropping to study her slim woman's body, curled half defensively against the corner of the sofa. He whispered, 'You're so desirable. So lovely.' He touched her cheek, his caress tracing the beautiful curve of her facial bones, following the delicate line of her jaw. 'So. You imagine I'd change you, Chris?'

'That's what you want to do.' She fastened her blouse with numb fingers. 'You don't really like any opposition. You hate it! You've never had an ounce of respect for anyone else's integrity, especially not mine. Do you really think I'd willingly give way, let you dominate me completely?'

'I see.' Brooding eyes studied the bitterness on her young mouth. 'Is that how you feel about me?'

'Yes!'

'And now you're despising yourself for responding to me? Because with me it was pure sex, without the roses and satin hearts?'

'I want to go home now,' she said in a low voice, hating the way he seemed to see right into her heart, knowing her most secret thoughts. 'I want to forget that this ever happened.'

'I don't,' he said softly. 'And if you imagine that it won't ever happen again, you're being very optimistic indeed.'

'It won't,' she said blindly. 'Not unless you want to be even more deliberately crude than usual.'

'Crude?' He mused over the word. 'If a man's desire
to make love to a woman he feels a lot for is crude—
then yes, I am a crude man. Because what I want right
now is to to carry you through to that bedroom, strip
you naked, and——'

'Stop!' she whispered, her palm covering that
passionate male mouth to silence the words that were
making her giddy. 'Don't say it!'

He took her hand in both of his, kissing her palm,
the fluttering pulse, the tips of her slim fingers. 'It's what
we both want,' he said quietly, black eyes meeting hers
with a shock that made her weak. The possibility was
all too close, and the need in her was becoming an exact
partner to his. A need to lose herself in the storm of
Nash's lovemaking, to give him the inner secrets of her
sexuality, let him transfigure her——

'No,' she said, the word almost a plea. He'd done this
before, probably with exactly the same words, and on
this very sofa, with dozens of others, Anita Klaus included. She was only the latest in a very long line of
women. A line which would continue long after she was
utterly forgotten. A tragic sense of depression flooded
her heart at the thought, and she struggled to her feet,
her eyes wet with unshed tears. Why did it have to be
her? She was so unprepared, so defenceless to him!

He rose fluidly, the gentleness in his face draining away
to leave the granite hardness of the Nash Canfield she
knew best. 'I'll take you home. Come on, for God's sake,
before I resort to the brute tactics you're always ac-
cusing me of.'

'You wouldn't.' It wasn't a challenge; she really did
know enough about him by now to know that whatever
other sins he might be guilty of, that wasn't one of them.
He wouldn't need force, anyway, she realised with a bitter

touch of self-knowledge, not with her—and he probably knew that, too!

'Your opinion of me must be rising,' he said with mock-astonishment. She stumbled on the threshold, clutching at his iron-hard arm and forcing a humiliating, 'Sorry,' out of her.

'No need to apologise.' He glanced at her downcast eyes. 'It's rather pleasant to see the ultra-efficient Chris Yardley looking less than her normal cool self. You look like a lost little girl.' A comforting arm slid round her shoulders. 'You'll sleep like a log tonight.'

In the Rolls she sat wrapped in silent thoughts. Back there, in Nash's apartment, she had learned something startling about herself—and about Nash. There was something in her that responded to him, older and deeper than any conscious thought. Nor could she deny what they both now knew—that she desired him, needed him.

And, on the other side, there was something in Nash that made him desire her. Maybe it was only the routine arousal of a potent male by an attractive woman who might, just might possibly, be conquerable. Maybe it was something deeper, some quality in herself that made him desire her for more sophisticated reasons. To crush what he saw as her challengingly cool efficiency, perhaps.

But, whatever it was, it changed the way she felt about him for ever. From now on, every time she caught those dark eyes on her, she would know that he might be desiring her. Exploring her body with his mind...

What a complex, baffling man he was! He combined some of the best and worst characteristics a man could have. Cultured, sophisticated, unbelievably generous at times; at times totally ruthless.

His life had been savage in parts, giving him an unflinching sense of purpose. Easy to use that as an excuse for his wicked ways! But he had none of the self-centred narrowness of almost every other man she'd known. He had a breadth of vision that made him stand head and shoulders above the herd. Yet it was that very masculine quality that grated on her nerves, making her as skittish as an Arab mare under a too-rough spur.

What was she going to do about him? She didn't have the temperament for love affairs, especially with a man as dangerous as Nash. And sex meant far too much to her to be simply given and taken as casual pleasure.

Like a salmon that had once been free, her spirit had been hooked, and she had the uneasy feeling that, no matter how she struggled, the dark man with the black eyes would slowly, steadily reel her in. Until she was utterly at his mercy.

'Do you mind if I ask you something?' Nash said casually, apparently concentrating on the evening traffic.

'What?'

'Whether there's anyone else.'

At first she didn't understand what he meant. Then she laughed miserably. 'You mean another man in my life? Whatever gives you that idea?'

'You seem very taken with a certain cinematic personality lately,' he suggested drily, flicking on the wipers to clear away snow.

She almost let her jaw drop. Duncan Anderson had been the last thing, the very last thing on her mind tonight. She was just about to say so, when it dawned on her that a lie might be very useful just now. When faced with an assault as devastating as Nash was capable of mounting, any defence was better than none at all.

'I don't know about Duncan,' she said, making her voice sound deliberately indecisive. 'He's very attractive, and he seems genuinely keen on me...'

Nash looked at her sharply. 'Are you serious?' She nodded silently, and his mouth twisted in what might have been scorn. 'Damn,' he half whispered. 'I didn't think it had gone that far.' She saw that his knuckles were white on the wheel. 'The man's a pompous, arrogant fool,' he told her grimly. 'I can't believe that you can really care for him!'

'You wouldn't have the remotest idea,' she agreed drily. 'He has a sensitivity that you lack utterly.'

'I don't lay claim to delicacy of feeling, Yardley. Unlike your Mr Anderson. But I do lay claim to common sense.'

'Duncan has something better. He's an artist.'

His eyes narrowed. 'The wild and woolly poetical type always does appeal to women,' he observed with fine irony. 'Are you trying to say you haven't seen through the man yet?'

'You talk as though he's some kind of charlatan,' she retorted. 'He's not—as you'll see when you meet him next Saturday.'

Bringing up Duncan's presence at Nash's party hadn't been very wise. She saw his jaw-muscles clench beneath the tanned skin. 'He must be over twenty years older than you,' he gritted.

'And I presume you're quite free of the cradle-snatching charge?' she enquired sweetly. It was nasty enough to make him curse.

Suddenly, Chris felt a great deal more self-confident! She was a lot more at home with the familiar Canfield-Yardley sparring contest than with the wildly turbulent emotions she'd felt back there at the apartment.

Her mouth was still bruised from his kiss. She touched it instinctively with her fingers, betraying her thoughts. It occurred to her with a flash of revelation that this was maybe what their mutual antagonism had always been about, right from the start—a way of evading the devastating attraction that smouldered between them, just below flashpoint...

Hastily, she shut that perilous thought away, and launched back on to the offensive.

'In any case,' she said with more than a touch of her old starch, 'Anita Klaus seems to be taking up rather a lot of *your* time. How was your squash game on Saturday morning?'

'Stimulating,' he said shortly. 'Sometimes I think she's more of a realist than you'll ever be.'

'No doubt she's more of everything than I'll ever be,' Chris said snappishly, not at all pleased that he was now taking swipes at her.

'At least she's had to make her own way in life,' Nash said harshly. 'She was born with nothing.'

'Like you,' Chris put in scathingly. 'No wonder you feel an affinity.'

'Yes,' he nodded, pulling up outside her house. The woods were dark and foreboding, dark as the empty windows of her own home. 'Yes, Anita is like me. She's had to work damned hard, and she respects the value of sound commercial sense. She hasn't had everything handed to her on a plate, the way you've had!'

Real hurt flashed through Chris, turning instantly to anger, and making her hands shake. 'Next to her, I must be downright insipid.' Her voice was unsteady again. 'In fact, I wonder why you bother with me at all. She's really far more your type.'

'Meaning?'

'Meaning that you and I come from different worlds, Nash.'

'You don't have to paint a picture,' he rasped. 'I'm a mercenary barbarian who destroys everything I come into contact with, showing no understanding of tradition or the finer things of life.'

'That isn't what I said—'

'It's what you meant.'

She didn't contradict him. But as she met his eyes, she was suddenly aware that she had hurt him.

Oh, he would never acknowledge it in a million years—and if she hadn't been in some kind of strange contact with him for that second, she might never have noticed. But somewhere, deep beneath those layers of armour-plate, she had cut into him, had cut into that wide-eyed paper-boy who had long ago dreamed of great things.

Yet her anger wasn't appeased yet. 'You don't understand me, my background, or my opinions. You never knew my dad, so you can't have any idea of the sort of man he was. Yet you despise his kind of journalism, you despise his standards—in fact, you despise and reject just about everything that's most dear to me. When I said we were like black and white, I meant it. You'll never understand me. Never! You're not capable of it!'

He lowered his head like a fighting bull, powerful and distinctly aggressive. 'I think that's enough, Christine.'

'Nor will you ever understand this town,' she went on, not caring that she was running headlong along a cliff-edge. 'You're a product of inner-city deprivation, so how could you appreciate the values that exist here? All you can see is the bank—and the red-light district!'

She'd gone too far, and his eyes were blazing. She reached out to touch his hand, opening her mouth to utter some foolish apology. But it was far too late.

He leaned across her, and threw her door open hard enough for it to rebound on its hinges. 'You'd better get out,' he said shortly, his voice like rusty hinges. 'And get back into your neat little suburban home, and nurse some of those neat little suburban sentiments.'

Snow blew into the car fiercely, but it was not as cold as his words. 'Nash, please——'

'You're perfectly right.' He cut through her wavering voice, his eyes stony. 'I don't know why I do bother with you. You deserve Duncan Anderson, every mangy inch of him. And if it arouses your prurient curiosity, Christine, I intend to go straight round to Anita's right now, and remind myself of what a real woman is like!'

Her eyes were swimming with tears as she stumbled out of the car and trudged through the thick snow to her garden gate. She hadn't felt so miserably alone and desolate since her father's death. Behind her, she heard the door slam, and the tyres skid as he accelerated away and into the snowstorm.

She was crying in earnest as she threw herself on to her bed. God, she felt wretched. *Bloody* man! She felt as raw as though he'd flayed every inch of skin off her back with those last few words.

An image of Anita's triumphant eyes swam into her mind, tormenting her with the thought of Nash in her bed, pouring his anger and desire into violent lovemaking.

It was too horrible to think about. Her body was still shivery from the emotions she'd been through, her muscles as weak as water. From the heights of passion, she had been plunged into an abyss of unhappiness. Thinking back to what had happened at Nash's apartment made it all the worse.

Had she ever experienced an arousal as intense as that? Chris didn't want to answer the question. It was as though he had left some secret chemical in her blood, a recurrent fever that would always explode into flame at his touch.

She reached for the telephone to call Jean, desperate for compassionate company this night, of all nights. But Jean wasn't answering. She was at her writer's circle, as she was every Monday.

So she went wearily to the kitchen, opened the fridge, looked dully at the food she had no appetite for, and finally settled for the cold comfort of corn flakes and a cup of tea. Please, she was praying, please let him not go to Anita tonight. She couldn't bear that.

The memory of the horrible things she had said to Nash burned her thoughts. How could she have been so cruel, so thoughtless? She'd deliberately struck at him to wound, and why? Because he had aroused her more than any other man had ever done? Was she some kind of frigid monster, striking out at the man who had dared to touch her heart?

She had an instinct, little better than a hope, that Nash and Anita had never actually been lovers. Not yet. But if Nash went to Anita tonight, then she herself would have driven him into her arms.

She dropped her spoon, ran back to the phone, and rang Nash's number, not knowing what she would say, just praying that he would be there, and not at Anita's. There was no answer.

And though she kept trying, again and again, every hour until midnight, getting steadily more miserable, there continued to be no answer from Nash's number. He hadn't gone back to his apartment. And she was forced to confront the implication that that entailed.

Tormented by the thought of what might have happened that evening, she kept rehearsing that horrible fight with Nash in her mind. Remembering the things

that had been said, regretting them as bitterly as she had
regretted anything in her life. Tears blurred her eyes as
she thought of all the things she could have said instead,
all the sensible things that might have averted this awful
night.

Maybe the pain she felt, as she finally crawled miserably into bed after midnight, should have taught her
something about herself; but for the present, Chris was
just too wretched to do more than allow her whirling
mind to ease into sleep.

# CHAPTER SIX

CHRIS could hardly bring her mind to bear on the conference next morning. Tom, Bob Jennings, and three people from her own team, including Jean, had squeezed into her office to thrash out the main elements of the Ransome Street article.

She had glimpsed Nash in his office earlier. He was looking rather grimmer than usual, but he hadn't noticed her. Or maybe he hadn't been interested enough to even glance her way. She had crept into her room with a lump in her throat, and buried herself in work.

At that precise moment, Tom was making everyone laugh hysterically by describing his encounter with one of the prostitutes' clients, but Chris either found it in such appallingly bad taste, or was so miserable, that she didn't even try and feign a smile.

'I don't find anything remotely amusing about this subject,' she said shortly, cutting through the laughter. 'We've all put in a lot of hard work, and now, as we don't have a great deal of time, can we stick to business?'

'Sorry,' Tom murmured, amusement fading from his face. 'What do you want to do with the statement Nash got from the commissioner?'

'I think we might use it as a theme,' Chris said tautly. 'Given the sub-editors' approval, part of it might do as a headline for the main story, too. It's certainly dramatic enough. There's also the question of this petition. Should we be involved in it in any way, or should we leave it up to the residents themselves?'

'That depends how we go on it,' Jean put in. "Nash obviously wants us to crusade, but——'

She broke off as the door opened, to admit the elegant figure of Anita Klaus.

Chris's nerves tightened as her eyes met the source of the interruption. Anita sashayed in, looking particularly ravishing in a figure-hugging green silk dress and matching stilettos, her stockings and other accessories in black. Nice outfit for Ransome Street, Chris felt with a flash of bitter anger, but hardly suitable for the offices of a newspaper. Thinking about last night, she could hardly bear to look at the tanned, feline face that turned her way.

But it was on her that Anita's dark, slanty eyes were fixed.

'Sorry to interrupt the scribes' congress,' she drawled, 'but I have the details of a big promo being done by Moon Pearl Cosmetics. They're keen on competitions, as you all know. Thought it might interest you, Chris.' She dropped the folder in front of Chris, and smiled down at her, one hand resting lightly on a svelte hip.

No one else in the room could see the look she was giving Chris. Which was just as well, because it was a look that held a message, a look that managed to combine malicious triumph with the purring contentment of the cat that got the cream. It meant only one thing, and Chris felt the blood drain away from her cheeks, leaving her cold and dead.

'Sorry to cut in,' Anita said in her husky voice. 'But I would really *hate* to think of you losing any more wonderful opportunities. You seem to have a penchant for that, don't you?'

She smiled down at Chris, gloatingly, pityingly, then turned on a green stiletto heel, and walked out. Leaving Chris feeling that she'd just been shot through the heart.

The atmosphere in the office was awkward. Puzzled amusement made Tom Shoals shake his head. 'That one's a queer customer,' he mused. 'I've never worked her out. What do you think the point of that was?'

'Just to show us her mouth-watering new outfit, maybe,' Bob Jennings shrugged. 'She looks like something out of a soap opera.'

But Jean was looking at Chris's white face with concerned brown eyes. 'Are you feeling OK, Chris?' she asked quietly.

'Fine.' Her voice seemed to stick in her throat, and her blood was like ice. So it happened. She'd managed to drive Nash into Anita's arms. She'd managed to lose him for ever. Focusing her mind away from her pain was the hardest thing she had ever done. 'Shall we get back on with Ransome Street?'

Losing something sometimes made you painfully aware of its value, long after it was too late.

When Chris next saw Nash, at the editor's table, she felt her heart contract painfully. She felt then that she had never seen a more beautiful, more complete man. He was laying down the law, using those glittering black eyes and that superb voice to make his points clearly and emphatically.

The others were listening with attention. Not with deference. Rather, with the instinctive regard of colleagues who trusted and respected—maybe even liked— a supremely competent boss.

It came to her quite suddenly that the resistance at the *Herald* had been largely in her own mind for the past few months. Yes, there had been suspicion and resentment at first. But not any more. Since Nash had proved himself, he had gained the respect and cooperation of everyone on the staff.

Except her own.

She alone, of all the people whose jobs had been saved, and whose futures had been secured by Nash Canfield, had continued to resist. She, who of all people ought to have put the good of the newspaper first, had stubbornly remained out of step, had pig-headedly and blindly continued to fight...

Hot with shame, she gathered the pile of copy in her arms, and tried to move past the open door without being noticed.

But Nash's voice reached out to her harshly. 'Chris! Will you wait a moment? I want to speak to you.'

She nodded dumbly, and waited in the babel of the newsroom while Nash made some final points, listened to further suggestions, then agreed on a final policy of presentation.

When he came out to her, he was unsmiling. This time there was no small-talk, no enquiry about her health, though his first glance at her pale face and reddened eyes would have told him clearly how she'd spent the night. 'You've got your act together on the Ransome Street story?' he asked.

'It's ready for you to take a look at,' she nodded. She'd put everything into this story. If he didn't find her work satisfactory now, there would be nothing left for her to give him, because she'd already given her heart and soul.

'We'll have to make it soon,' he said shortly. 'We're both going to be busy. Be in my office at three this afternoon.'

'OK,' she said, lifting unhappy grey eyes to his, then dropping them again.

'Elliot Seddon will be there as well,' Nash informed her unemotionally. 'He's rather concerned that the lay-out and presentation of your section haven't shown much flair lately. I agree with him.'

As a rebuke, it was a mild one, but it brought the fresh blood rushing to her cheeks. He didn't seem to notice, though. In the same flat voice, he went on, 'About next Saturday night. You'd better go down to the florist's and the restaurant tomorrow morning to ar-range things. I'd prefer it if you could get all that done as early as possible.'

'Yes,' she nodded. So she was still expected to hostess in ten days' time. That was something, and it took a little of her misery away. But the way Nash was dealing with her indicated that little more than an armed truce was to exist between them. There was nothing in his manner to suggest that she was anything more than an employee, like any one of fifty others on the staff.

He hadn't mentioned her Duncan Anderson in-terview, which she'd finished, and which was now ready for his desk. It was hardly a diplomatic moment to bring it up, but if it was to go into the Wednesday Review, he would have to see it this afternoon. She mustered a little courage.

'The Anderson interview's also finished,' she told him. 'Do you want to see it?'

That had been a mistake; she realised it at once. His eyebrows came down like storm-clouds, and his mouth hardened to a grim line. 'You can forget that,' he said harshly. 'I'm spiking it.'

'Until when?' she blinked.

'*Spiking* it,' he repeated impatiently. 'Not postponing it. You can put it in the bin.'

Hurt made her cry out. 'Why? It's one of the best things I've written, and it's taken days of my time to get done!'

'It's not topical,' he ground out. 'Considering that the national crisis is still unresolved, and considering the amount of important foreign news coming in, there's no room for self-indulgent interviews with minor movie-people.'

'How do you know it's self-indulgent when you haven't so much as looked at it?' she demanded. The wastage of copy in any newspaper was prodigious, she knew that well enough. But this, she felt instinctively, was sheer spite on his part, and that made her already frayed nerves jump. He'd already had his revenge for last night with Anita. It was cruel to axe her perfectly good article into the bargain! 'Duncan Anderson is a major talent, not a minor movie-person. And I'm not a cub-reporter. To send me on time-consuming assignments just to spike my work is plain frivolous.'

Nash's eyes narrowed, dark, slitted windows on raw anger within. 'Don't you lecture me on what is or isn't frivolous,' he rasped. 'You seem to have some peculiar notion that you carry some weight around here, Yardley. You damned well don't. You may have been something special in this newspaper once, but not any more. You've sold out to me, remember? And, right now, you're just a cog in a very big wheel. If you value your job, try not to forget that.'

He pushed past her, stony-faced, walked across to his office, and slammed the door behind him. She stood in stunned misery, stared at by the two or three people who'd caught some of Nash's reaction over the clatter of the typewriters. She felt her self-control crumbling like a sandcastle at high tide. Blindly, she walked through the newsroom and out into the corridor. The only place she knew she could be alone right now was in the printing-room.

It was almost empty, except for two technicians doing routine maintenance on the vast presses. From the rooms beyond came the usual sounds and voices of the type-setters, busy setting up the evening edition. The printing staff were almost a tribe all to themselves within the newspaper hierarchy. Intent on their own business, they paid her no attention at all as she sat on a bench and sank her head into her hands.

What had gone wrong with her life? She'd been so self-assured, so poised until a few weeks ago. Now, all she could think of was Nash Canfield. And the sense of loss she now felt was so acute that she almost didn't want to go on.

She leaned back, inhaling the so-familiar smells of ink, oil, and newsprint, this machine-room bouquet that had such a curiously comforting effect on her tired nerves. She was facing a central problem. Was she a woman first—or a journalist first? Did she want to go on working for Nash, irrespective of her personal feelings towards him? Or did she want to get away from him, get away to a fresh start somewhere a long way away?

For the hundredth time, thoughts of resigning drifted through her thoughts. Maybe now, more than ever, was the time to go. Leave it all behind her, and make a new life for herself. Embrace London, and a future that just didn't include this town, the *Herald*, or Nash Canfield. That would be so simple, cutting through the Gordian knot of her multifarious problems at one stroke.

Or was it too late, after all? Too late to leave Nash, too late to try and cauterise him out of her heart?

'Why so pale and wan, fair lady?' Duncan slipped an arm round her shoulders, and squeezed her tight, his lips brushing her hair. 'I think that man works you far too hard. Come on, drink up, hmm? A little wine will do you good.'

'Oh...' Grateful for Duncan's comforting presence, Chris smiled at him wearily. 'Sorry, I'm drooping like a lily. Today was especially fraught.'

'I can see why.' She had brought Duncan the late edition of the *Herald* when she'd come out to meet him at this wine-bar. It was a new place, all pink plush and soft lights, with smooth jazz oozing out of the piano trio on the tiny stage, and the ambience, as Duncan would have called it, was certainly doing wonders helping her unwind.

She was very glad Duncan had called her at work to ask her out tonight. A little company was exactly what she had needed to restore her spirits. She hadn't told him about Nash spiking the interview yet; that could wait until some more opportune moment, later on tonight. Like after she had issued the invitation to Nash's dinner-party, for instance.

She drank the sweet German wine, and sighed with contentment as the band launched into a silkily paced swing number, straight out of downtown New Orleans. 'I like this band.'

'You look lovely tonight,' he said, his eyes flattering her figure. And despite her weariness, she *was* looking good. She hadn't worn this dress more than once since she'd bought it. Straight-fitting Chinese printed silk, with a slash neck and a black belt, worn over a filmy blouse, with red wedge-heeled sandals, it had a distinctively Suzy Wong air about it. Her platinum hair was swinging free, silky and fragrant from her shower. 'Thank you, kind sir,' she nodded graciously. 'I like that jersey of yours. You didn't buy that in England.'

'Hollywood,' he said smugly. 'Cashmere. Cost me a bomb, too.' In his white polo-neck and slacks, he looked a great deal younger than he had done in tweeds or a suit. The more stylish clothes suited him better, matched his image as a movie-maker better, too. For the first time, she was noticing Duncan as a physical presence—as a man, rather than as a mind. And Nash had been wrong. Duncan was certainly not old, and very far from mangy!

'Anyway,' Chris apologised, 'All this has been an interruption. You were talking about your new American film.'

'Yes—and probably boring you to tears.'

'Not at all,' she pleaded. 'Please go on, and don't mind my vacant expression. I *was* listening.'

His eyes crinkled warmly, and he covered her hand with his own, stroking her knuckles with sensitive fingers. 'Funny, I feel as though I've known you all my life. The moment I set eyes on you, I felt something spark between us, Christine. Something very special.'

'Oh, Duncan,' she smiled, finding it hard to take him seriously, 'you're just trying it on.'

'I assure you from the bottom of my heart that I am not. Know who you remind me of? Zara. Zara Zoffany, my great discovery for *Starfire*!'

'Except that Zara's seventeen,' Chris pointed out wryly, 'and I'm twenty-six. I'm over the hill already.'

'Don't be absurd!' His eyes darkened at the mocking way she talked about herself. 'You know,' he said seriously, 'there might even be a future for you in pictures. I mean it. You have such a beautiful face, like a Renaissance angel. And that hair, like spun silver! And your hands are so beautiful, Chris...' Looking deeply into her eyes, he lifted her hand to his mouth, and kissed the satiny skin with warm lips.

'Well, well, well!'

Chris stiffened in horror. She would have known that deep voice anywhere in the world. And when she and Duncan both turned to look, Nash Canfield was standing over them.

With Anita Klaus smiling wickedly at his side.

'What a pleasant coincidence,' Nash said, his voice a velvety purr. He was radiating elegant charm, his smile wide as a tiger's.

It would have taken someone who knew him very well indeed—like Chris—to tell by his eyes that he was very, very angry.

'Mind if we join you?' he said, making it more of an order than a suggestion.

'Not at all,' Duncan conceded, though slightly stiffly. He let Chris's hand drop. 'Let me guess—you're Chris's boss?'

'Indeed. And you're Duncan Anderson?'

'Mmm. We were just talking about you, Mr Canfield.'

'Yes?' The two men were sizing each other up. 'It didn't look to me as though you were talking about anything much—except each other.'

It was an appalling situation. Gulping her heart back out of her throat, Chris composed herself enough to intone introductions at that point. Nash towered over Duncan like a hawk over a rabbit, but the greeting he gave was friendly enough.

Only those black eyes, glittering anger, gave anything away. 'This is my advertising manager, Anita Klaus,' he presented Anita. Anita didn't even bother to do more than smile. She just wrapped both hands around Nash's arm, and hummed along to the music, smiling at Chris with slitted, slanting eyes.

Sick to her heart, Chris wondered how in God's name the evening was going to turn out. It was hard to say which was worse—being caught by Nash, having her hand kissed by Duncan, or seeing Nash out with the clinging Anita. If she could have rubbed a magic lamp at that moment, and instantly consigned both Anita Klaus and Duncan Anderson to an identical wine-bar on the other side of the world from Lancashire, she'd have done it without hesitation.

But Duncan had recovered from his initial resentment at being interrupted over Chris's hand. Nash's air of apparent friendliness seemed to have soothed him, and they all sat down on the plush pink velour with the usual platitudes. Uncomfortably, Chris found herself cornered by Nash on one side, and Duncan on the other, with Anita directly opposite—a more than slightly claustrophobic situation to be in.

Oblivious to any of the tensions that were swimming around like dangerous undercurrents beneath a calm sea, Duncan gave Nash a friendly smile. 'So when is Christine's interview with me going to be printed?'

Nash's eyes met Chris's with an ironic glitter. She was absolutely dreading his reply.

'Quite soon,' he said easily. 'As soon as we have a suitable slot.'

Relief flooded Chris. Duncan was wagging his finger at Nash, a familiar gesture. 'Don't leave it too late, mind. It's going to be brilliant stuff.'

'Oh, no doubt it'll be totally riveting,' Nash said smoothly. Thank God, Duncan's ego was too big for him to notice any sarcasm. Nash nodded to summon the waiter over, and ordered champagne—a Bollinger. 'We'll want something special to toast our celebrity guest,' he went on. 'Congratulations on the Film Society awards, by the way. You've done very well with *Starfire*.'

Duncan Anderson smiled a touch smugly. 'So they keep telling me. But I assure you, I certainly wasn't aware of doing anything out of the ordinary when I was making it.'

'Duncan's busy with a new film,' Chris put in hastily, to change the subject. She sensed a disaster looming somewhere in this conversation, and she was desperate to avoid it. Anita, thank God, hadn't made a contribution yet. Flushed with her victory maybe, and feeling herself in a completely unassailable position over Chris, she seemed content to just smile sweetly at Chris and cling to Nash's arm. It wasn't easy to take, but at least she'd refrained from any overt nastiness.

'Oh?' Nash raised an interrogative eyebrow. 'Along the same lines as *Starfire*?'

'No, no. A director can't stay in the same place for ever, Mr Canfield. I'm always moving onward.'

'So I see,' Nash nodded, his eyes flicking to Chris momentarily. 'What's the subject?'

'Ah. I was just telling Christine that it's rather confidential.' He beamed at Christine, and gave her hand a squeeze. Nash's dark eyes followed the movement, and lifted to her own with undisguised contempt. Feeling her skin crawling with embarrassed horror, Chris worked her fingers free from his grasp and tucked both her hands under the table, away from danger. 'But I can tell you this much,' Duncan flowed on, 'it'll be a savage indictment of modern society.'

'Indeed? That sounds fascinating.' Only someone who knew Nash's poker face really well would have been able to tell that he meant just the opposite.

The champagne arrived at that point, and in the fuss of popping the cork, pouring, foaming, and mutual toasting, the little gathering took on an unreal air of *bonhomie*, like a forced Christmas party.

Chris had always loved champagne, but right now it tasted like wormwood—especially when Anita lifted her glass at her with a deliberately mocking smile.

'So you enjoyed *Starfire*?' Duncan enquired, smiling over his glass. 'I'm very glad. Did you see it, Anita?'

'Yes,' Anita said. 'It was a beautiful film. I cried at the end. And,' she added in typical Anita fashion, 'it's been a sound commercial success—I believe it's doing very well at the box-office.'

'I believe so,' Duncan said modestly. He turned back to Nash with eyes that were eager for more praise. 'But did it really deserve a British Film Society award? Come now, Nash, you're obviously a man of judgement. Do you think *Starfire* really warranted the "best movie" accolade?'

'You want my opinion?' Nash asked easily.

'Your *honest* opinion.' Duncan nodded brightly. 'Don't hold back, now.'

It suddenly dawned on Chris with a pang of alarm that Nash had set Duncan up for the perfect bring-down. But it was too late to intervene.

'In my honest opinion, then,' Nash said, '*Starfire* won the award principally because all the other films of last year were so poor.'

Duncan's smile evaporated. 'I thought the competition was pretty fierce, myself,' he said shortly.

'Oh, there's no question that a lot of people liked *Starfire*,' Nash conceded smoothly. Ignoring Chris's murderous look, he went on with that maddening Cheshire-cat smile of his, 'But then, they would do. It was mildly erotic, jejune, sentimental pap—and that always sells, doesn't it?'

Chris closed her eyes in horror. She didn't know what 'jejune' meant, but she knew what sentimental pap was.

'How dare you!' Duncan's voice was quivering with outrage, and Chris could hardly blame him. 'I thought you were a man of taste!'

'I like to think I am,' Nash said languidly. 'But *Starfire* didn't taste of anything much to me—unless it was milk and water.'

'That's your expert opinion?' Duncan retorted with furious sarcasm. 'And you call yourself a newspaper editor!'

'You wanted it straight.'

'I didn't want insults!'

'We'd better start getting ready to go,' Chris said hastily, trying to salvage the wreckage of a rapidly disintegrating situation. But no one offered to get up to let her out of the corner she was wedged into. She grimaced silently at Nash. Dismay was a feeble word for what she was feeling right now. Even Anita was looking appalled, her glass frozen on its way to her lipsticked mouth.

Nash merely smiled a little wider, black eyes hooded as they surveyed Duncan Anderson's face. 'The film was beautifully made, I grant you that. But it was little more than a showcase for the adolescent talents of Zara Zoffany, wasn't it? And since her talents seem to consist mainly of staring into the lens with swimming eyes, I'm afraid I got rather bored after the first half-hour.'

'What *is* this?' Red-faced and spitting, Duncan spun round on Chris. 'What are you going to write about me in your article? God, have I let myself be set up for some nasty little hatchet-job?'

'Nash's opinions are very different from mine,' Chris said, giving Nash a positively savage look. What on earth was he doing? 'I happen to think *Starfire* was a brilliant film, and I've said so in my article.' She tried to soothe the quivering director. '*Starfire* deserved every award it got, Duncan. It's a great film, your triumph in fact.'

'I liked it too,' Anita put in. 'I said so.' Her eyes flicked to Nash. 'At least, I—er——'

In another situation, it might have been comical to see Anita so torn between wanting to follow Nash's lead and not wanting to offend a VIP. Right now, it was anything but funny.

'Let's go,' Duncan said abruptly, and rose to leave, his green eyes bulging. But Nash leaned forward, his expression amused.

'Mr Anderson,' he said gently, 'I have to apologise.'

Duncan glared at him suspiciously. 'I bloody well think you should!' he snapped.

'I was having you on,' Nash said contritely.

'Having me on?'

'I'm afraid it's a very wicked ploy of mine. When I really like something, I deliberately attack it in order to test my own opinion. I have to confess I was doing that with you.'

'Are you telling me you liked the film after all?' Duncan queried darkly.

'That's exactly what I'm saying,' Nash agreed. He was using the sort of soothing voice a vet might use on a fretful parrot, but, astonishingly, it seemed to be working. Duncan's ruffled feathers were almost visibly settling back into place.

'You've got a damned peculiar way of showing your appreciation,' the director muttered. 'I've never heard anything like it.'

'I'm sorry,' Nash said, and his actor's voice was beautifully modulated to express contrition, reasonableness, kindliness; you would never have guessed he'd just ripped Duncan's masterpiece into bloody fragments. 'I should never have said all that. But I always find that if something survives really harsh criticism, then it has supreme quality. Please sit down, Duncan, and have another glass of champagne, and I'll tell you what I really think about *Starfire*.'

Duncan subsided back into his seat. He was looking far from pleased, but that hypnotic aura of Nash's seemed to be exerting a spell over him. Nash, Chris thought bitterly, was deliberately manipulating Duncan's emotions in the most Machiavellian way—and in front of Anita, too.

'I am very touchy about my work, Mr Canfield,' Duncan said petulantly. 'My feelings are much more highly tuned than other people's. I have an extremely sensitive nervous system, I'm afraid. You journalists can't imagine what I go through.'

Ignoring Chris's tight expression, Nash eased into his most charming style. 'Don't get me wrong, please. I respect your stand over your work. You're a truly great artist, and, like all artists, you have your integrity.'

'Well——' Duncan bridled, mollified.

'And *Starfire* really is a wonderful film,' Nash pressed on, bringing a beam to the director's face. 'The way you portrayed a young girl's awakening to love—marvellous. Really profound. Only someone with a truly sensitive nervous system could have produced it.' If any irony was present, it didn't register with Duncan, who was actually preening himself by now. 'I'm really looking forward to discussing the film with you at my party,' Nash continued. 'It's rare for us to get an artist of your calibre in our midst.'

'Party?' Duncan echoed. 'What party?'

'Hasn't Chris conveyed my invitation yet?' Nash said in surprise. 'That was remiss of you, Christine.'

'I was going to do it tonight.' Her silvery eyes were dancing with anger. 'But perhaps you'd better ask him yourself?'

She sat in taut silence while Nash explained about the distinguished dinner-party he was planning, and secured Duncan's acceptance. He'd got Duncan into a delighted mood by now, the fury of a few minutes ago completely forgotten. But, right now, Chris was almost hating Nash.

Neither Anita Klaus nor Duncan himself probably realised what that had been all about—but Chris knew, very well. It had been a sophisticated little game on Nash's part. A carefully staged, and probably planned, exercise designed to demonstrate exactly how much control Nash could exert over Duncan. And in the process of showing his own mastery, to show Chris just what a childish and vain fool Duncan Anderson really was.

Well, he might have done all that. But Chris, far from being impressed, was raging against him inwardly.

Of course Duncan had faults as a character! But none of it took away from his very real talent as an artist. And it merely confirmed the very worst aspects of Nash's character—the manipulative, ruthless side of the man. How *dared* he interrupt her evening with Duncan? How *dared* he insult her companion, make a fool out of him in front of everyone? It was intolerable.

And what was even more intolerable was seeing Duncan now purring under Nash's flattering words, his face expressing pompous self-satisfaction. Didn't he realise what Nash was doing to him? She'd never really contemplated Duncan as a lover for one second, but Nash didn't have to go to these lengths to demonstrate how unsuitable he was . . .

Anita had now unexpectedly joined the conversation. Even the mention of the dinner-party, to which she hadn't been invited, didn't seem to have dented her self-satisfaction in the slightest. And her respect for the ability to make money was keeping her attitude towards Duncan deferential—or maybe she was just following her lord and master's lead? Either way, the atmosphere was now transformed. Except in Chris's little corner.

She sat without contributing more than monosyllables while Nash, Duncan and Anita talked animatedly about films, newspapers, and the media in general.

The attack now over, Nash was like a panther after the kill; claws in, purring with affable *bonhomie*. You felt you could almost reach out and stroke those sleek muscles. Everyone seemed to have forgotten that blood was ever shed at this table.

But not Chris.

Yet she had to admit he was superb at what he did. She'd never seen Nash in this kind of setting, and she had to admit that it was an education. The jagged edges of that powerful personality were now smoothed to an elegant poise. He was witty, sophisticated, almost wickedly polished; and yet there were traces of the traditional Nash Canfield to add spice to the playboy smoothness.

After a while, the conversation turned around to Nash's own acquisition of the *Herald*, and his background in newspaper publishing. A few of the stories he told, about the days when he'd mixed with toughs and criminals on the poorest streets of London, ran fairly close to the bone, but Duncan rocked with appreciative laughter, and, despite her simmering anger at the way he'd behaved tonight, Chris found these glimpses of the inner Nash all too fascinating.

'So there is some truth to the story that you were a gangster,' she said drily over the second bottle of Bollinger.

'Well, it was touch and go for a year or two,' Nash said with a smoky smile at Chris. There was underlying seriousness in the dark eyes, though, that told her he wasn't just teasing this time. 'I hadn't had much of an example to live up to. Half my friends were bent in some way or another.'

'And you?'

'I was poor and ambitious, and that's like petrol and fire—an explosive combination. For me, it was either pull myself out of the gutter the hard way, or take the deceptively simple path of street crime.' He leaned back in his chair, the beautifully cut suit he wore an odd contrast to the pictures his words evoked. 'It would have been so easy to knock some old lady down, steal her purse.' He was talking to Chris alone now, midnight-black eyes touching her soul. 'Throw a brick through a jeweller's window. Climb a factory wall one rainy night. And that would have been it. The rest of my life would have been as predictable as——' He smiled. 'As the bill that will shortly land on this table.'

'Why didn't it happen?' Anita asked, her slanty eyes intent. Nash's tales had obviously excited her, and Chris could bitterly see the fascination in her pretty face.

'Fate,' he shrugged, turning to Duncan. 'As an artist, Duncan, you know the part that fate plays in our lives.'

'As an artist, I know the part character plays in our lives,' Duncan said firmly. 'I don't think you could ever have been a common thug, Nash. Crime just isn't in your character.'

That was all *he* knew, Chris snorted inwardly. As if reading the mental remark, Nash lifted an ironic eyebrow at her. 'Hear that, Chris?' Nash said with an ironic gleam. 'Some of my staff might disagree with you, Duncan.'

'I'm sure that even if Nash had turned to crime,' Chris suggested sourly, 'he wouldn't have been a common thug. By now he'd have been running London's underworld.'

Nash's laughter was genuinely amused. 'Sometimes I think Chris knows me better than I know myself. Should we make real pigs of ourselves, and order another bottle?'

'This is costing you a fortune,' Duncan beamed. 'But why not? You two seem to get along like a house on fire.' He winked at Nash. 'She's always talking about you.'

'Is she?' His eyes met Chris's with a hidden irony that maybe only the two of them could appreciate. Then he said softly, as if no one else were in the room, 'Chris has more in common with me than she realises.'

Flushed with irritation, Anita started talking again, slightly too loudly, defusing the moment of tension. Soon, it was forgotten.

But Chris found herself thoughtful as she sipped her champagne, aware that her head was already swimming a little. Something in common? For God's sake, what?

She and Nash could scarcely have had more different upbringings. She had known every luxury, at least until she was sixteen. She had been raised in the shadow of an impregnably respectable newspaper. She had gone to school with girls who had grown up to marry into the wealthy, fox-hunting, county set. Before the final traumatic bust-up, her home life had been privileged and sheltered. She had read incessantly, been exposed to culture from an early age.

Nash had, by his own admission, barely opened a book until his twenties. His mother, whom he charitably described as a 'popular lady', had evidently not been the caring kind, and neither she nor Nash were any too sure who his father was. In any case, she'd abandoned him very early to pursue her own life, and he had been educated on the streets, his personality hardened by knocks and sharpened by hunger.

Maybe that was why she was hidebound by codes and conventions—like not telling Duncan to his face that his work was junk—and why Nash just didn't give a damn about things like that. To her, 'doing the right thing' had always come paramount, even higher than success or failure, winning or losing. Nash wasn't like that. Nash was a winner. An achiever. Nash Canfield was of the breed that leads others, possessing the ruthless vision necessary to ensure the survival of all.

And the rest followed in his wake—continuing to survive by virtue of his efforts, while luxuriating in their scruples and finer feelings.

What did she have in common with a man like that? Somehow, his words had struck a chord with her. She did have something in common with him, but what? He was so different from her. Everything he had, and he now had real wealth, was the product of his own fierce drive to succeed.

And yet you'll always be hungry, she thought, lost in the intensity of her own vision of Nash. 'For all you could buy half the restaurants in town today, Nash, you'll always be hungry.'

She looked up suddenly to see all three of them staring at her curiously.

'What did you say, Christine?' Duncan asked in puzzlement. Her face flaming as she realised she must have spoken aloud, Chris could only stammer a confused apology. 'I—I was thinking of something else. Please don't pay any attention,' she begged.

'Maybe Chris has had too much champagne,' Anita suggested kindly.

'Maybe I have.' Chris smiled with an effort. 'What were you saying, Duncan?'

'I was just talking about my days at film school,' Duncan said, launching into the topic with relish.

The conversation was familiar—she'd heard much of this from Duncan already—but Chris was painfully aware of Nash's dark, thoughtful eyes on her, and she was damning herself for being such a fool. As a child, she had often done that, involved herself so deeply in her own thoughts that she had spoken them aloud. It had been years since that childhood habit had resurfaced, though.

She met Nash's unfathomable gaze, and flushed all over again, feeling her body respond to him in tightening nipples and a shiver of gooseflesh. Blast! Looking into his eyes always ignited that potent reaction in her. Ninety-nine per cent of the time it was obscured by simmering tension. But the other one per cent of the time it was something else, something deep-rooted and primitive that she didn't even want to recognise.

An hour later, the wine-bar started to fill noisily with people coming out of films or plays, and, by mutual consent, their party broke up.

Nash didn't volunteer where he and Anita were going next. But then, he didn't have to. Anita's sultry smile at Chris made that perfectly clear, and Chris felt the old, sick pain start throbbing inside her.

'See you next Saturday, at my apartment,' Nash nodded to Duncan. 'Goodnight, Chris.'

'Enjoy the rest of the evening,' Anita added sweetly. 'I'm looking forward to your next film, Mr Anderson.'

The goodnights were over in seconds, and Chris found herself watching Anita and Nash walk away towards the Rolls-Royce, a glass splinter of pain jammed into the sinews of her heart.

'They've got style, both of them.' Duncan was watching Anita's swaying hips, Nash's elegant prowl. 'Are they lovers?'

Chris tore her eyes away from Nash's broad-shouldered figure, and tried to keep her voice normal. 'I don't know.'

'Funny,' he volunteered, 'I really can't work out whether I like that man or hate him!'

'Don't you? I wish my feelings were as uncomplicated as that.'

Duncan laughed loudly. He had drunk a lot of champagne, and his grip on her arm was distinctly amorous. 'Don't tell me you've got a crush on him? He's old enough to be your father.'

'He's only ten years older than I am.'

'Ah, I keep forgetting, you're twenty-six.' He kissed her neck, breathing boozy fumes across her face. Chris felt nothing, not even distaste. 'You look so very young— young enough to be one of my own kids.'

'Your kids?' she asked shortly, looking at him with cool grey eyes.

'I assure you,' he smiled, 'my feelings towards you are anything but paternal.'

She evaded another kiss. 'How many children have you got—as a matter of interest?'

'Three.'

'*Three?*'

'I don't see a lot of them,' he said airily. 'I feel they have to find their own way in life without a lot of paternalistic interference from me.'

'Without your responsibility, you mean?'

'Sweet,' he said, his smile fading to something more sour momentarily. 'For God's sake, Chris, I only fathered them. Fiona gets plenty of money from me to bring them up. I've got my own life to lead!'

'Indeed,' Chris said drily.

'Any case,' he pointed out, 'do we really have to discuss my boring family affairs on the pavement?'

'No.' Chris waved down a cruising taxicab. Dear God, what an immense gulf existed between this man and Nash Canfield! She could just imagine the expression on Nash's face if he had heard that. To a man like Nash, having a family represented the most ultimately important thing in his life. A family meant people to be loved, cherished, cared for with every fibre of his being— not an irritating encumbrance to be shrugged off as soon as some other flirtation presented itself.

Suddenly, Duncan's image as the witty champion of liberated sexuality seemed just so much tarnished tinsel.

'Anyway,' Duncan said expansively, 'I suppose I can give you all the gory details back at the farmhouse, eh?'

'I suppose you could.' The cab pulled up, and she opened the door for him. 'Get in,' she invited.

'Age before beauty, eh?' he laughed, and climbed inside obediently, peering out at her. 'Where are we going next?'

'I'm walking back to Woodside,' she informed him, and shut the door firmly on him. 'You're going home by cab.'

'Hey!' He wound down the window, and stared out at her with wounded eyes. 'The night is yet young——'

'Not for me,' she said shortly. 'I'm exhausted, Duncan, and I've drunk far too much bubbly. I'll call you over the next couple of days.' She gave Duncan's address to the taxi-driver, and he pulled off obligingly.

The last she saw of Duncan was his betrayed face hanging out of the window, still trying to talk to her. At the corner of the street, Nash's Rolls pulled out behind the taxi, and both cars disappeared in the direction of Market Square.

Feeling desolate, she pulled the collar of her coat up against the cold night air, and started her walk home. So much of life was just a shallow show. So little was real.

She had a great deal to think about.

# CHAPTER SEVEN

THE edition of the *Herald* with the Wednesday Review in it, despite the thousands of extra copies which Nash had ordered printed, proved to be a sell-out.

On street-corners, in newsagents', in the railway and bus stations across the county, the newspaper sold to the last issue. And on Friday afternoon, requests were still coming in for back copies.

Not that Chris was in any position to be concerned about sales at that stage. She was far too busy. The feedback that had come pouring into the Wednesday Review offices was stunning.

Some of it had been outraged complaint that the good name of the town had been dragged through the mud. But by far the biggest proportion of letters and calls had been supportive. Everybody most directly concerned with the problem—the social workers, most of the council, but above all, the local residents—was pleased that the situation had finally been brought to light. The general reaction was summed up by a Ransome Street resident, a lady in her seventies, who rang Chris late on Friday afternoon.

'Thank goodness someone's finally had the courage to tell people what goes on here,' she said vehemently. 'Now maybe something will be done about it!'

It was, Chris reflected wryly as she rang off, another Nash Canfield triumph. But Nash himself had disappeared on a mysterious mission to Manchester that morning, leaving the deputy editors in charge. Missing his day of glory, she reflected.

What she didn't bank on, though, was that it was also becoming a Chris Yardley triumph. Several friends had already called to congratulate her on the standard of the journalism.

And when she emerged from her office at five, she was greeted by a party of old *Herald* hands, including Timothy and Jean, who presented her with a framed picture. She studied it with amusement. It was a cartoon of her, drawn by Willie Roper, the *Herald*'s resident cartoonist, depicting her as an armoured Joan of Arc figure, doing battle with a hydra-headed monster in fishnet stockings, labelled 'The Ransome Street Dragon'.

'Hail to the heroine of the hour,' Timothy grinned. 'The Mayor's just been on local radio making a public pledge to get Ransome Street cleaned up in two months. Get your helmet on! We're taking you down to the Grapes for a drink.'

Listening to the congratulatory uproar in the little pub that had always traditionally been the journalists' hangout—the printers drank at the Magpie round the corner; executive staff went to Francois's wine-bar—Chris felt more than a pang of shame at her own initially uncooperative and unenthusiastic attitude on the Ransome Street story. She didn't deserve all this, not really.

Somebody, slopping his pint over her elbow, announced, 'The Wednesday Review comes of age. Out of bloomers and pigtails at last!'

'I'll drink to that,' Timothy nodded. 'Here's to Chris, who's just confirmed herself as a serious journalist with something to say, and something to contribute.'

Chris felt her cheeks flaming as the glasses were raised. She was moved by the compliment, but she couldn't help still feeling that she was undeserving of it—at least in spirit.

'None of it was my idea,' she protested. 'I just produced what the editor wanted. The idea was all Nash Canfield's.'

'That's the editor's job,' Timothy smiled. 'To see the newspaper in his mind's eye. Your job is to *make* the newspaper. And you've certainly done the *Herald* proud this time.'

'I didn't care for the story at all,' she went on, still trying to make a public confession of her unworthiness. 'I thought Nash was all wrong about it at first.'

But no one was listening any more.

'You've got strong opinions,' Timothy nodded, pitching his voice below the noise of conversation, so that only she could hear. 'A good reporter has to have opinions, Chris, and if he believes his editor to be wrong, then he has to have the courage to say so. But there's also such a thing as editorial policy, and it's part of your duty to fall in line with it.' He scratched his iron-grey thatch of hair. 'To tell the truth, you've had me worried at times. I thought you were never going to accept Nash's leadership. There were even times when I thought you were considering resigning from the *Herald*.'

'At times, I was.'

'But not any more?'

'I think I've just started realising how foolish I've been. And it may be too late now.' Chris stared into her glass in silence for a long moment, thinking of Nash, and Anita Klaus, and what might have been. She sighed heavily. 'I miss Dad sometimes. But Dad's...'

'Sam's dead,' he finished for her. The words were not brutal, but they were firm. Timothy drained the rest of his pint. 'Sam's dead, and Nash is in his place. And

Nash is a damned good editor. It's a privilege to work for him.' He glanced at her. 'I think you're just beginning to realise that, aren't you?'

'Yes,' she nodded, 'I think I am.'

'I'm glad. He thinks the world of you, and it's a shame to see so much potential unrealised. Stick with him, Chris. He'll take you a long, long way.'

The reason for Nash's absence on Friday became clear on Saturday evening. Jean, who'd picked up the news from one of her contacts in Independent Television, telephoned Chris at home to tell her to watch the News at Ten.

She saw it at her grandmother's house. The item was slotted into the financial news section, and had come from a Manchester studio.

'On Friday afternoon,' the pretty young newscaster announced, '*Sunday News* board officials applauded the acquisition of the paper by *Lancashire Herald* owner-editor Nash Canfield. The price paid for the ailing newspaper—now said to be losing half a million pounds a year—was a princely twelve million pounds. Canfield has made the *Herald* pay in just six months. Can he do the same with the *Sunday News*? With me in the studio is Nash Canfield himself.'

The camera cut to Nash, looking calm and poised in a charcoal suit. On television, his dark good looks and formidable authority had massive impact. Chris felt her heart squeeze at the sheer presence of the man.

'Mr Canfield,' the interviewer was saying, 'today we've heard accusations that you're planning a newsroom bloodbath at the *Sunday News*, in order to save profitability. Is there any truth in that?'

'None whatsoever,' Nash said curtly. 'I've negotiated a voluntary redundancy scheme with the various unions involved. There will also be a re-shuffle in some departments, but not among journalistic staff. Apart from that, I have no immediate plans for a radical staff change.'

'How, then, are you going to make the *News* pay?'

'If you want an idea of my style of management,' Nash replied, 'then take a look at the *Herald*. I haven't had to sack anybody there.'

'You're currently editor of the *Herald*,' the interviewer said, changing tack. 'I assume that keeps you fairly busy on a day-to-day basis. How are you going to be able to give both papers your full attention?'

'I'll have to make certain obvious personal changes to take account of my new situation,' Nash shrugged, giving nothing away.

'Does that mean you're going to appoint a new editor for the *Herald*?'

'I didn't say that.'

'So what changes can we expect in the *News* from now on?'

For the first time, Nash smiled. 'You can expect a paper that's interesting, stimulating, informative and exciting. Buy it next Sunday, and see.'

The girl's mouth curved in an answering smile. 'I'll look forward to that. Finally, Mr Canfield—the *Lancashire Herald*, and now the Manchester *Sunday News*. Are we seeing the start of a newspaper empire?'

'I don't think so. I'm content to just run my two papers the best I can for the time being.'

'I don't know whether to believe *that*.' The girl smiled. 'Thank you, Mr Canfield.' She nodded, and turned back to the main camera to continue with the financial news.

Chris got up to switch the television off, and glanced at Dorothy. 'What do you make of that?' she asked in awe.

'I make a very rich and powerful man,' her grandmother said, watching Chris's face. 'What he told that girl was just flummery, take my word for it. In ten years' time, Nash Canfield is going to be owning a dozen papers, and probably not just in this country, either. He's young, formidably intelligent, and he's got the push to do it.'

'That means he'll leave the editorship of the *Herald*, then,' Chris said. 'Isn't it ironic? Dad's precious news-paper was just the first stepping-stone for Nash. And I used to get so het up about it.'

'Will he be able to make the *Sunday News* pay?' Dorothy asked.

'No question,' Chris nodded. 'He's very brilliant at what he does. And there's an opportunity for him to make a great deal of money out of the *News*.' She sat in front of the fire, hugging her knees and watching the flames in the grate. 'He'll probably leave the *Herald* before the spring,' she mused.

Suddenly she was contemplating something that had always seemed like a dream to her—a *Herald* without Nash Canfield. Except that it was suddenly more like a nightmare now.

God, she thought with a twist of pain, life was going to be so empty without Nash. She had a vision of herself, working away at her Wednesday Review for the rest of her life, caught between the walls of the *Herald*, while Nash soared upwards and onward, leaving her behind him for ever.

Life without Nash. It hardly bore thinking about. It was like imagining a life without sunshine, an existence without stimulation or pleasure of any kind. In the absence of Nash, life had no savour. She had only half realised it in these past few weeks, but Nash Canfield had come to be the centre of her existence. Whether she loved him, or whether she hated him, it was impossible to say. But life without him was going to be very meaningless...

'Are you going to miss him?'

'There's going to be a very big hole,' Chris sighed. In the firelight she was as pretty as a painting, the flames touching gold into her silver colouring. 'I've come to...rely on him being there.'

'That's a funny statement, coming from the girl who was always threatening to resign.'

'I know.' She closed her eyes. 'But I don't know what I'll do without him.'

'Oh?' Gran smiled. 'I got the impression that life with Nash Canfield was one long struggle.'

'It's been like that today, at any rate,' Chris snorted. 'I was at the florist's first thing this morning, ordering God knows how many white lilies. And then straight over to Nash's apartment with the manager of Wenham's. No Nash on hand, of course—he's in Manchester, whipping the *News* staff into line. Which leaves me to arrange a five-course meal for fifteen people. Waiters, wines, food, the lot. It's going to cost him a fortune,' she added with grim satisfaction. 'There's that consolation, at least. I deliberately picked the very best.'

'He'll obviously expect it,' Dorothy commented. 'If you'd wanted to upset him, you should have economised.' Her eyes were unexpectedly shrewd. 'Are you in love with him?'

'In *love*?' Chris was taken aback. 'Of course not!'

'Well, you're in something with him,' Dorothy Yardley said drily. 'Maybe it's time you found out what—for your own sake.'

On the drive home to Woodside, that word 'love' kept haunting Chris's thoughts. It was a word that had meaning for her, but not maybe the meaning it had for other people. As a teenager, she had dreamed that love could be a tempest of passion that would sweep her off her feet and change her life for ever. Well, her parents' divorce had changed all that. In the desolate aftermath of the separation, she had learned just how empty a concept it could be.

There had never been any shortage of men to take her out, and she enjoyed socialising. Yet she'd also kept all of them at arm's length. There was a wariness about Christine Yardley, an unwillingness to commit herself to anyone. Love belonged in films like *Starfire*. As far as she was concerned, her career gave her all the satisfaction she wanted out of life.

And that brought her back to Nash. Everything in her life seemed to bring her back to Nash, as though she were caught on a wheel that had him as its hub and centre. This evening's revelation had been a shock. Dorothy was perfectly right; Nash had a long, long way to go in life. He was not going to remain editor of the *Herald* for long. And the depth of her own feelings about his departure had shocked her.

What was the feeling she had in common with him? Something she couldn't name. And how would she survive without him? She was simply unable to contemplate existing without Nash there to infuriate her, to goad her, to drive her.

But if that wasn't love, then just what *was* it?

\* \* \*

'Well then, can you tell me why on earth you chose to insult Duncan in front of all of us, and make him look a fool?'

'It didn't take me to make Anderson a fool. The man's mother did that for him, fifty years ago.' Unrepentant, Nash rose from his desk and stretched like a leopard studying a tasty young gazelle. 'And it annoyed me to see him slobbering all over your hand.'

Annoyed him? The cheek of it! 'You aren't my keeper,' she snapped.

'Then maybe I should be.' He moved to her, reaching out to brush the long, platinum-bright hair away from her face, making those ripples of reaction shudder down her spine. 'Would you care to be my kept woman?' he murmured, those deep, sexy eyes holding hers.

'That isn't funny.' With an effort, she pulled away from him. 'I've given the material to Elliot Seddon,' she informed him coldly. 'He's checking to see whether there's enough *flair* in the presentation.'

She turned to go, but he moved easily into her path as she made for the door, and halted her by taking her arms in strong hands. 'What's got into you, Chris? I wasn't *that* rude to your cinematic boyfriend.'

'Yes you were!'

'Did I dent his little ego, then?' he said contemptuously. 'I hope you rubbed it better for him.'

'Now *that*,' Chris said, shimmering with anger, 'is just nasty.'

He cocked his head to stare at her with those hard black eyes. 'Is it? Haven't you taken on the job of massaging the Anderson ego full-time?'

He was utterly hateful! '*You* should talk! You seem to relish having Anita Klaus fawning all over you!'

'Yes,' he drawled, 'I do, rather.'

'Pig,' she said, quietly but furiously.

'Careful.' His fingers tightened their grip on her slim arms. 'You might just talk yourself out of a job.'

'That might just be a relief.' She really didn't care whether she was sacked, suspended or promoted right now. Without Nash in the editor's office, the *Herald* wouldn't have the slightest shred of interest for her, anyway. 'Please let my arms go. I think I'm losing the circulation in my hands.'

'You'll live.' But he relaxed his fingers, as though remembering his own strength. It was hard to read whether he was amused or angry. Perhaps he was both. 'I was pleased with the Ransome Street story, by the way,' he said. 'You're showing promise at long last.'

Pleased! After she'd slaved her heart out for him! 'Oh, thanks,' she said with scathing irony.

'Yes, it was good. I didn't get a chance to tell you before the weekend,' he smiled.

'No.' Her amethyst eyes met his with a dry glint. 'You were too busy buying up half of Manchester's newspapers.'

'Just the one,' he said gently. 'I needed something to do over the weekends.'

'I thought you were planning on being such a devoted family man?'

'Oh, I am.'

'You were bad enough as owner of the *Herald*,' she said shortly. 'With two newspapers to contend with, you'll be like a bear with a sore head. I'm glad I won't have to see it.'

His eyes narrowed, a hungry Red Indian lining up on a deer. 'And why won't you see it, pray? Going somewhere?'

'No, but you will be.'

'How do you know that?'

'Simple logic. You won't have time to edit the *Herald* any longer; you'll be too busy administering your acquisitions. So you'll appoint another editor here. And after that,' she said with a note of bitter accusation, 'I'll never see you—*we'll* never see you—except when you come down to bully the new editor.'

A slow smile crept across the finely chiselled mouth, as though light had just dawned on him. 'So that's what's biting you!' He considered her from under thick lashes. 'Are you going to be lonely without me, Chris?'

'Not in the slightest,' she said with cutting emphasis. 'In fact, it'll be a lot quieter round here, while you ascend the ladder of success.'

'Play your cards right,' he said mockingly, 'and I'll take you with me.'

'I don't want to come, thanks,' she said briskly. 'Take Anita, instead.'

'I'm taking her in any case,' he said smoothly, and Chris felt her cheeks flush red. Giving him a furious glance, she pushed round him, and opened the door.

'Chris, do me a favour——'

'Yes?' she ground out, turning.

He was watching her with inscrutable eyes. 'Don't waste your time with Duncan Anderson.'

'I'm not wasting my time,' she told him silkily. 'He's quite serious about me.'

Nash's eyes glittered. 'All he's serious about is getting you into bed.'

'Well, why not?' Only real, deep anger could make her answer him back like this. 'It might be fun.'

He took two steps towards her, and the stormy look in his eyes frightened her. 'You little——'

'Go on,' she invited bitterly, 'I thrive on insults.'

'Did you know that he's married?' Nash said in a voice choked with anger. 'That he has three children?'

'As a matter of fact, I did,' she said with a brittle smile. 'Is that the best you can do?'

The savage expression on Nash's face deepened. 'I suppose you approve of Mr Anderson's thoroughly modern life-style?' he asked grimly.

'I don't pretend to judge him,' she retorted. 'Unlike you, I feel that his life's his own business.'

'*His* life? What about his wife's life, which he's effectively ruined?' Nash's powerful hands clenching at his sides. 'What about the lives of his three children?'

'None of that is my business. Or yours. And you don't have any damned right to tell me who I can or can't associate with!'

'All I'm concerned with,' he retorted hotly, 'is what's best for you.'

'Well, thank you for your concern,' she told him with wounding coldness, 'but I don't need your advice. I think you should stick to your own little affair with Anita Klaus, and stop prying into my private life.'

For a moment she feared he was going to strike her, and she flinched from the look in his eyes. 'Get out of here,' he said, the quietness of his voice worse than any shout.

'I'll be glad to.' As she walked through the clatter of the newsroom, Chris was trembling with angry emotion. For two pins she was ready to hand in her notice this minute. Damn him! He was getting more and more impossible to work for; who did he think he was? Right now, she didn't care whether she never saw him again.

It was definitely going to be advisable to keep strictly out of Nash Canfield's way until the party!

* * *

'I suppose you must have met Nash for the first time when he offered to buy the *Herald*,' Petra Stonehouse asked.

'That's right.'

'What did you think of him?'

'He terrified me,' Chris smiled. 'But I knew that if I didn't sell to him, the *Herald* didn't have a hope of surviving.' She looked round quickly, checking that glasses weren't in need of filling.

Dinner was going to be slightly awkward, Duncan Anderson's inclusion meaning that there would be an odd number at the table; but that was not a crucial issue. What was important was that people enjoyed themselves, and there seemed no question about that. Nash's dinner-party was turning out a brilliant success; the fifteen people seemed to be enjoying the evening without exception.

Most of the guests were local, and so Chris knew them, at least by reputation, but Sir George and Lady Stonehouse were among the few people here, apart from Chris herself, who were not strangers to Nash.

The Stonehouses seemed to be really fond of Nash, and Chris had been longing to talk to them and get their opinion of Nash off the record.

'We've known Nash for ages,' Petra Stonehouse said in response to Chris's questioning. 'Nash came to George for financial advice when he was first starting to make money—oh, it must be fifteen years ago, now. George was so impressed with this bustling lad, because that's really all he was, that he brought him home for dinner. Frankly, Nash looked as though he could do with a square meal in those days.' She smiled wickedly. 'He's filled out a little since then.'

'Hmm.' Chris glanced across at Nash's big, powerful figure, so potently attractive in evening dress. He was being the perfect host, charming and urbane. Hard to imagine he could be such a pig when he wanted. She was still simmering with anger against him, but she was keeping it well under control tonight. You couldn't win by letting him get to you.

'Aha! I thought I'd lost you.' It was Duncan, bearing champagne, and Chris groaned inwardly. Though she'd been doing her best to pair Duncan off with some of the other guests, he'd been sticking to her apron-strings—ivory *crêpe de chine* wrapover blouse, black skirt, Indian silk scarf tied round her taut middle—with embarrassing dedication.

'You never finished telling me about your next film,' Petra Stonehouse complained.

'Ah, but it's confidential, dear lady, quite confidential.' Nevertheless, he was as eager to talk about himself and his work as ever. Nor did the fact that Chris had already heard most of it twice prevent him from including her in his audience, making it hard for her to break away.

His green eyes drifted across her bust as he talked volubly. He seemed fascinated by the outline of her breasts against the ultra-fine silk; and, considering that every time she met Nash's eyes there was a very obvious reaction for Duncan to study, he was staring with an intensity that deepened with each glass of champagne. Irritating, but she had more poise than to cover her telltale nipples by folding her arms. Duncan wasn't to know that another man entirely was producing the peaks that so intrigued him!

It was fully fifteen minutes before he'd finished his lecture about his next film project, by which time Petra,

eyes slightly glazed, was obviously eager to fade away—
which she did with aplomb, leaving Duncan to corner
Chris again.

'You fascinate me,' he said huskily. 'You elude me,
Chris, you evade me. But how long can you keep on
running?' He grasped her hand amorously. 'When will
you face your own feelings?'

She caught Nash watching them across the room, his
eyebrows tilting ominously downward at the sight of
Duncan clutching her hand. Good, she thought wickedly.
Let *his* blood pressure rise for a change, even if there
was hell to pay later!

'Come on,' she invited sweetly, smiling at Duncan a
lot more warmly than she really felt, 'I want you to talk
to Heinrich von Kleist. He's one of the most amusing
people I've ever met.'

'I don't want to be amused. I want to stay here, losing
myself in the immense depths of those cool grey eyes of
yours.'

'You're being silly.' Knowing it would infuriate Nash,
she allowed Duncan to clasp her arm possessively as she
led him across to Heinrich, and was rewarded by a murderous glint in Nash's black eyes as he turned away.

*Good.*

The massive sitting-room was, even if she said so
herself, a splendid sight. As she had planned earlier, she
had arranged the chairs in roughly three conversation
areas, so as not to split the party up too much.

The flowers from Osprey's, a fortune in tall lilies,
added an air of opulent grace around the room; and
when she'd last slipped off to the kitchen, the Wenham's
staff had been preparing the dinner for exactly a quarter
to nine. Already, fragrant aromas were to be smelled,
indicating that all was being brought to readiness.

Nash had very much left it all to her, not interfering with her decisions, simply enjoying the end product with appreciation. For all his high-powered life-style, Nash knew exactly when and how to delegate, and how to relax!

Across the room, someone was asking Nash about the *Sunday News* purchase.

'There are several possible advantages to having a Sunday as well as a weekday paper,' he replied. 'One of them is co-ordinating very expensive services, like foreign coverage. Another option may be sharing the presses, which would effectively make us a seven-day newspaper.'

'And reduce costs correspondingly?'

'Of course,' Nash smiled.

'You're an absolute pirate, darling!' The comment came from Ella Bricknell, a pretty redhead who'd been hanging on Nash's arm for the past hour, apparently without annoying her husband, a local MP as well as being a substantial landowner. 'An absolute sea-wolf, isn't he, everyone?'

'You're certainly causing a stir in the marketplace.' Sir George Stonehouse, tall and distinguished, lit a cigar and watched Nash shrewdly through the resultant smoke-haze. 'I take it the *News* will have to change fairly radically if it's to become profitable, Nash?'

'You mean on news policy? Yes. The *News* is very old-fashioned, and it's lost almost half a million readers over the past six years. A few very simple changes, along the lines of what we've done with the *Herald*, will make an instant impact to start with.' Fleetingly, his eyes met Chris's, making her drop her gaze. 'Slightly bigger headlines, bigger body type, shorter and terser articles, bigger and better pictures—that'll all help. But the

*Sunday News* also needs some purely financial muscle, and I'm assembling a team for the job right now.'

'A hit-squad?' Sir George enquired, lifting a bushy eyebrow.

'More a blood-transfusion,' Nash replied. 'It won't be a very big team, but I flatter myself I know how to pick the very best.'

'Does the best include Chris Yardley?' The shrewd question came from Petra.

Nash smiled his Cheshire-cat smile. 'I have other plans for Chris,' he purred. His eyes were on her again, with an expression that made her weak at the knees. She looked down at her watch. Saved by the bell. 'I think,' she decided, 'that it's just about time for dinner!'

There was a general rising in response to her words, and Nash touched the button that slid the dining-alcove door open. The expert staff had been busy. Rose candles were flickering in the silver candlesticks, and the staff were poised to serve the first course.

Conversation divided into two general camps—those at Nash's end of the table who were talking about the newspaper publishing world and the big business in general, and those at Chris's end, who were talking more generally.

Duncan had been placed opposite Mary Maconochie, an attractive woman of around his own age, and he was at last making an effort to talk to someone other than Chris—which enabled Chris to get Petra Stonehouse talking about Nash.

'He's the mainstay of the St Martin's Home, you know,' she was telling Chris. 'It's one of his and George's pet charities.'

'The St Martin's Home?'

'It's a London children's home. What used to be called an orphanage. Hasn't he ever said anything about it?' And when Chris shook her head dumbly, Petra nodded. 'Oh, yes, he's been funding them for years. He obviously feels very deeply for young people growing up without parents, the way he did. It was Nash, in fact, who got George involved. They give shelter to homeless children, and try and find them good foster-homes.'

'I never knew,' Chris said ruefully, some of her pent-up anger melting a little. There was a great deal that she didn't know about Nash, it transpired. She listened in silence while Petra described Nash's involvement with the home, painting a picture of a caring, compassionate man, very different from the ogre she'd once imagined him to be.

'What was he like as young man?' she asked Petra curiously.

'As a young man? He's not exactly ancient now.' Petra smiled. 'Well, I suppose at fifty-nine I think anyone in their thirties is a mere baby.' She dissected her hors d'oeuvre thoughtfully. 'He was quite unforgettable, actually. He had tremendous maturity and confidence for his age, but there was something else—an urgency, a thrusting quality that set him right apart from any other man. You could tell he was going to go a long, long way. I don't think that quality in him will ever change.'

'I don't think so either,' Chris agreed. She couldn't take her eyes off Nash. Two images of him were flickering in her mind, like a split-screen movie. One of the Nash she knew, giving her sheer, unadulterated hell at the *Herald*. Another of the Nash she could only guess at, giving his time and money to help children whom life had treated with less than compassion. They were images hard to square with one another.

She signalled for the main course, a roast of pheasants, grouse and quails with fresh winter vegetables.

Someone beside her, who'd been following her conversation with Petra Stonehouse, marvelled, 'How on earth did he ever make it from the slums to all this?'

'God knows,' Petra smiled, glancing across at Nash and catching his attention. 'How *did* you do all this, Nash? I was telling Christine about the days when you were glad to get a square meal at our table. Now you're worth God knows how many millions.'

'Oh, I'm a determinist,' Nash said with a slow smile. 'I believe that anyone can get anything he wants—if he tries hard enough.'

'And have you got everything you wanted?'

'Not yet.' He looked directly into Chris's eyes. 'But I have hope.'

'It's not that easy,' Chris said shortly. 'I believe that in this life you take what you get!'

'And I believe,' Nash said, flame flickering in his eyes as he stared at her, 'that in this life you take what you want.'

Petra Stonehouse chuckled at Chris's side. 'George and I have worked out an intermediate philosophy. In this life, you take what you can!'

Through the laughter which followed, Nash was still looking into Chris's eyes. 'If I want something badly enough,' he said, so that only she could have followed his meaning, 'I'll get it. In the end. That's all that matters.'

'Whatever your beliefs, Nash,' she said coolly, 'you'll find that some things are simply out of your reach.'

'I doubt it,' he said softly. 'I doubt it.'

Compressing her lips tightly, Chris signalled for the next course.

# CHAPTER EIGHT

IT WAS not until the early hours of the morning that the party was drawing to a happy, contented conclusion. If Nash's aim had been to establish himself as a force to be reckoned with in this town, he'd certainly done so. None of the people now making their way to cars and taxis was likely to forget Nash's charm, or his formidable intelligence. Chris had seen him forging links with the most influential and important people in the district—just as her father had once done—taking his rightful place as owner of two large local newspapers.

Mary and Duncan were the last to go, in separate taxis. At his taxi, Duncan took Chris in his arms, planting a rather alcoholic kiss on her mouth. She struggled free.

'Come back to my little farmhouse in the woods,' he whispered. 'It's full moon, and I want to celebrate!'

'You've celebrated quite enough,' she smiled, evading another kiss.

'You wouldn't regret it, I promise you!'

'I'm very flattered by the invitation,' she assured him, 'but I must help Nash do some tidying.'

'Nash, always Nash,' Duncan said angrily. 'You're not in love with the man, are you?'

'Not in the slightest,' Chris sighed, wishing he'd get into the taxi and leave now.

'I couldn't bear it if you were,' he said in a low voice. 'The man's mad about money and power. He'd crush you, my love.'

'It's very late,' she said firmly, repulsing another attempt to kiss her. Making Nash jealous was all very well, but she'd had enough now. '*Goodnight*, Duncan.'

As the black taxi pulled away down the smart mews that backed Nash's apartment, Nash himself walked up to her, a tall, dark figure with a cheroot smoking between his fingers.

'Have trouble persuading lover-boy to leave?' he asked laconically.

'Not in the slightest,' she retorted. 'He just wanted me to go with him.'

Nash raised an eyebrow. 'And did you accept?'

'Here I am,' she shrugged for an answer, slipping her hands into the pockets of her skirt and cocking her head at him. He grunted, taking her arm as they walked back up the stairs.

'He's fallen for you like an adolescent boy.'

'Adolescent?' she asked innocently.

'You know damned well it's only sex.' It was said in a husky growl that brought shivers to her skin for some reason. 'I don't understand why you allow him to paw you like that.'

The chance to irritate Nash was too good to miss. She pretended to consider, grey eyes absent. 'Maybe I rather enjoy being pawed by Duncan. He's very sexy, after all . . .'

Nash swung her to face him so violently that she gasped, her hair swirling platinum in the moonlight.

'You little——' She had never seen him look so angry; the expression on his mouth made her heart pound. 'Are you amusing yourself by playing with me?'

'I—I don't know what you mean,' she faltered, shrinking back.

'You know exactly what I mean. You know I want you—or, if you don't you're a bigger fool than I took you for. Sometimes you make me——' He broke off, clenching his teeth.

Was he really jealous of Duncan? The idea was so preposterous that Chris almost laughed. She wanted to tell him that the whole notion was ridiculous, that if there was any man in the whole world she felt any real emotion for, it was Nash himself. But before she could speak, he had taken her arm in a painfully tight grip, and was leading her unceremoniously up the stairs.

'You're hurting,' she said angrily. 'You've been such a good bear all night; what's given you a sore head now?'

'You,' he growled, but his fingers relaxed, leaving five spots of flame on her fine skin. 'Tell me,' he said roughly, yet pleadingly, 'is there anything between the two of you?'

'That isn't your business, Nash,' she retorted briskly. 'I'm not going to answer questions like that.'

'Then there is something,' he said, more quietly. His eyes narrowed to smoky slits, as though something had just seared his skin. 'I should have known better.'

'I'd say that you don't have the slightest evidence for either conclusion.' Her hands were shaking again; he had that effect on her when he looked like this. 'I'll help you tidy up, and then I'd like you to take me home, please.'

He stared at her for a few seconds longer. Then his face relaxed, and he laughed softly, tossing his cheroot like a shooting-star into the garden. 'I never thought I'd be making a fool of myself like this over any woman,' he said, taking her arm again. 'And I never thought you'd turn out a flirt.'

'Me, a flirt? What about you?'

He made an impatient gesture. 'Let's not waste time and energy arguing.'

'Oh, I'm very sorry,' she said acidly. 'I should just patiently wait my turn, I know. Is Anita starting to bore you? Is that why you're wanting to line me up? And who'll be next, when you're finished with me—Ella Bricknell?'

'Don't be so juvenile,' he said sharply.

'I saw the way Ella Bricknell kissed you goodnight,' she accused hotly. 'You just can't resist a pretty face. I'm surprised her husband doesn't shoot you with one of his matched Purdeys!'

'I know how he feels,' he said shortly. 'But as it happens, I'm one of the few men he really doesn't have to worry about.'

'Huh!'

'You do realise,' he said conversationally, 'that this is the third quarrel we've had tonight?'

She didn't think he wanted an answer to that. There was almost nothing to do to the apartment. Wenham's staff had left it spotless, and even as they walked into the living-room, someone had just finished vacuuming the carpets.

For something to do while Nash let the staff out with generous tips all round, Chris plumped a few cushions and mourned over a little china figurine which had somehow been broken. But her part of the evening was over now. She'd done her duty, and now she wanted sleep. That was all.

Or was it? Nerves were bunching inside her as she listened to the staff departing, the front door closing, the Wenham's van driving away into the night. Funny that, getting her jitters at the end of the evening, rather than at its beginning...

She flinched as she felt strong hands span her taut waist appreciatively. 'You're as delicate as a butterfly,' Nash said softly into her ear. 'Or should I say wasp? Sometimes I think you'll just float away on the breeze.'

'I'm not that light,' she assured him, trying to steady her voice.

'Oh, yes you are.' Effortlessly, he lifted her off the ground, making her gasp, then put her down and turned her to face him. 'But you've got a nasty sting, Chris.'

'So have you,' she shot back bravely.

His hands slid down shamelessly to her hips, pulling her close to him. 'Ever hear about the attraction of opposites?' he asked with a wicked glint.

'Tell me,' she invited ironically—and perhaps unwisely!

'It's when two people are crazy about each other but can't help fighting the whole time.'

'That sounds like hooey to me,' she said, her heart thudding heavily against her ribs. She met his gaze as fearlessly as she could. 'If they really were crazy about each other, why on earth should they fight?'

'Because they've got something in common.'

'What?'

'It.' He grinned, devastatingly handsome. 'What makes the world go round.'

She shook her head in denial. 'When two people are always at each other's throats, it's a sign that they're totally incompatible.'

'There's only one answer to that,' he threatened, eyes starting to smoulder.

'What's that?' she asked huskily, though she knew perfectly well that he was going to tilt her chin up, lean down, and——

This time she was reaching to slide her arms round his neck, her mouth opening of its own accord under that sweet onslaught. She was hungry for his kiss, aching for him, like she'd been aching all evening. It had been torment to have to look at him across the table, wanting him, trying not to show it, trying so hard not to admit to herself that she was falling helplessly under Nash Canfield's animal magic!

His hands slid down her back as their kiss deepened, pulling her close until her breasts were crushed against his chest. It was so good to admit her need for him at last, to simply drink in the passion he was offering her without question, to let the excitement run like wildfire in her blood.

Nothing mattered now, not the *Herald*, nor Duncan Anderson, nor Anita Klaus...

Nash pulled her down on to the sofa, fingers reaching for the silken knot that secured her blouse. 'This thing's been driving me crazy all night,' he said roughly. 'I could hardly listen to that empty chatter for thinking about how I would untie it, and...' His eyes were almost fierce as the silk rustled aside, revealing the hardening peaks of her upward-tilting breasts. 'God,' he whispered, 'you're so beautiful, Chris. The most beautiful woman I've ever seen.'

She moaned, helpless, as he kissed the ivory skin, tasting her, teasing the tight buds of her nipples into an ache of excitement. She found her fingers running through his thick, dark hair, hair that smelled so good, hair that was crisp, inviting her fingers to pull. His mouth became almost cruel with desire, making her gasp. Did he have any idea what he was doing to her?

Of course he did. He'd done this so many times before!

And yet she didn't care. In a crazy way it made it somehow easier for her to respond to him, realising that she was only the latest in a long line. That way it couldn't deepen into anything. Couldn't become serious, setting her up for the kind of hurt she dreaded.

And yet—dear God, how sweet it would be to believe that he really did care for her! It was her instinct for self-preservation that kept her sane, kept her hopes dormant in her heart. The terrible thing was that what Nash was doing to her was sending shock-waves exploding through her deepest, most hidden dreams. Dreams of love that she'd long since imagined dead. Dreams of children, of a wonderful marriage, of a relationship that could contain everything that was wonderful and great.

He had pulled his shirt off, and she was lost in the smooth, tanned wonder of his skin. So strong, so taut with potent male power! The hair across his chest and flat belly was black, black as sin, crisp under her fingers.

'Chris . . .' She could feel the tension in him, as though he were struggling with some overwhelming force inside him, having to restrain himself from simply taking her, here and now. The thought made her weak, frightened and yet confused beyond relief. It had never been like this with any man in her life before, not remotely like this maelstrom!

'Chris, are you all right?' His thumb brushed wetness off her cheek, and she realised that she was crying, her eyes blinded with tears.

'I—I'm fine,' she said unsteadily. The woman in her was reeling, the rules she'd been living by all these years in ruins around her. She clung to him as he comforted her with astonishing gentleness. He smelled clean, male, wonderful. 'You must think I'm such a drip,' she choked against his warm skin.

'A terrible drip,' he said gently, running his hands through her silky hair with infinite tenderness. 'Anyone would think you'd never done this before.'

'I haven't,' she said in a small voice. 'In case you haven't guessed ... I'm a virgin.'

'I have to admit that I'm glad to hear it.' Nash smiled against her temple. 'Or is that arrogant male chauvinism?'

'Everything you do is arrogantly male,' she accused, but there was no spite in the words. They were almost said in awe of him. She raised herself, aching, and looked at him with eyes that were soft as mountain mist. 'Sometimes you behave as though you owned the whole world, Nash.'

'All I want to own is you.' She could see the desire flickering in his eyes, and it struck her to her soul.

'But you can't own me,' she said, her voice almost hysterical in her need to convince herself. 'We've got nothing in common! We hardly know each other!'

'Then why are you letting me touch you?' he asked softly, fingers trailing across her skin. 'Like this ... and this?'

She had no answer, only a shudder of ecstasy that told him all he wanted to know. How *had* he broken through her defences like this? She stopped his hands with her own, her slim pale fingers closing round the rugged bronze of his.

'Don't,' she pleaded, her mouth trembling. 'If you want to show you can dominate me, there are other ways of doing it. Not like this ... I couldn't bear it!'

'Dominate?' He was smiling as he kissed her bruised lips. 'You really think I'm some kind of savage, don't you, Christine?'

'No, I don't. Once, maybe—but not any more. You're——' She tilted her head in sad bafflement. 'You're a mystery to me. So civilised in some ways, so ruthless in others...'

'Is that so mysterious?' Nash shook his head slowly. 'You've always tried to see me as a two-dimensional figure, Chris. Try remembering that I'm a man, with a man's heart and mind. You know what kind of childhood I had, you know what I've had to overcome. Maybe that's left me with some rough edges, some contradictions that I'll have to try and overcome. But it's also made me very sure of what I want in life. And what I want, more than anything, is you.'

'But why?' His intensity frightened her. 'Just because you think I'm a challenge to you?'

'For God's sake,' he said in disgust, 'get rid of all that "challenge" rubbish. I'm not talking about a quick affair! I'm talking about living together. A life together.'

'Me?' she asked, stunned. 'Here?'

'Is that such a terrible notion?' He kissed her parted lips, and she held him close with numbed hands, her heart pounding so wildly that she wondered he couldn't hear it. 'I want to get you out of that lonely house of yours. I want you here, with me, every minute of every day. I want to love you like you've never been loved in your life before!'

'I don't believe it.' Stupid words, but the only ones she could think of to say as she clung to him. How could she have dreamed that he was planning all this?

Or had she really known, all along, in her secret heart, but had lacked the courage to admit she knew?

When he'd told her he needed her, he hadn't just wanted her talents. He had been talking about *her*, the whole of her. 'I don't believe it,' she whispered again. 'You want me to become your mistress?'

'Yes.' He kissed her again, slowly, lingeringly, then smiled. 'I most certainly do want you to become my mistress. If that's all I can get for the time being, I'll settle for that. But in the end, my love, you're going to become my wife. And have my children.'

'I don't believe it.' She pushed away from him in a kind of panic. 'What are you *saying*?'

'I'm saying marry me,' Nash said gently.

Disbelief made her gasp, as though the oxygen around her had run out. 'Nash, it—it wouldn't work in a million years!'

'I was thinking of more like a few months.' He kissed her throat, his mouth trailing warm fire down to her breasts.

'You must be crazy!' Or was *she* crazy? Why else was she holding him so close, the tears pricking behind her eyes again? Why else was her heart in her throat? 'I can't understand why you're saying all this!'

'You really had no idea of the way I felt?' He smiled wryly. 'Not the faintest inkling?'

'I——' She struggled to be honest with herself. 'I thought you desired me, yes. But I thought that you also disliked me, the way I——'

'The way you disliked me?' he finished for her as she broke off in confusion. His mouth took on an almost bitter smile. 'I suppose it's better to have the truth. You still dislike me?'

'No,' Chris told him in anguish. 'But you must let me think, Nash. I'm not prepared for all this. I still can't believe that you're serious. And even if you are serious,' she rushed on, putting her fingers on his mouth to delay the angry retort she saw forming there, 'what hope would there be for any relationship between us? We fight like cat and dog as it is! I've seen my parents' marriage break up, at close quarters. I couldn't bear to have my own marriage go the same way!'

'My parents weren't even married at all,' he reminded her matter-of-factly. 'And divorce doesn't exist in my vocabulary, I'm afraid. I have no intention of breaking my children's home up.'

'Nash,' she pleaded, 'I've never even considered children, let alone marriage—let alone marriage to you!'

'You make it sound like something extraordinary,' he said laconically, watching her with dark eyes.

'It is something extraordinary. I'm just not the woman for you. You need someone...someone who shares your outlook on life, who shares your strength.'

'You do share my outlook, if only you knew it,' he retorted. 'And as for strength, Chris, you have more than your share.'

If only it were true! Exhaustion washed over her, reminding her of her own arguments earlier this evening— there wasn't any use in fighting against Fate, and she had a feeling at the pit of her stomach that Fate was going to deliver her into Nash's arms in the end. Struggle? Fight? That's what Nash would have done; but she was so tired. The relationship between them had always been a battle, right from the start. Now the battle had swung so far his way that she just didn't have a hope any more.

So much for her resolution to give him the fight of his life! Marriage to Nash. Would it really be the hell she imagined? Couldn't it just as easily, given a shift in the way she saw him, be a slice of heaven?

'Will you tell me something?' she asked, looking at him with eyes darkened with doubt.

'Anything you want to know,' he smiled, brushing the tumbled blonde hair away from her face.

'Have you ever wanted to marry—any other woman?'

He stared at her for a moment, then laughed softly, huskily. 'You still haven't worked it out, have you?'

'Wh-what?'

'There haven't been any other women. Not like you. *You* are my woman, Christine. And I'm going to marry you, because there'll never be anyone else.' He kissed her parted lips, tasting the salt of her tears. 'Silly girl. I only want you.'

She surrendered to his kiss. In a world which had suddenly become so uncertain, so confusing, the hard strength of Nash's body was a rock to cling to. And though disbelief was still numbing her mind, there was one thing he had said which she believed utterly and without question.

He wanted her.

In the arrogance of his will, he had chosen *her*. God knew the why or wherefore, but Nash's wasn't a personality given to falseness or indecision. His desire for her was as potent and certain as the sea.

She was melting against him, the tenderness of her response drowning every other thought. Another few moments, and she wouldn't be going home tonight. Nash would be making love to her, right here and now!

'No more,' she begged painfully. 'I must get back.'

'Do you imagine I could let you go now?' he threatened, eyes amused, passionate.

'If you don't, I swear I won't even consider marrying you,' she promised, panicking. He released her, and she pulled her blouse closed over her achingly sensitive breasts, feeling how powerfully her body was yearning for Nash's love. In the insanely unlikely eventuality of her ever marrying this strange, dark man of hers, one thing around which there could be no doubt would be their sex-life. She didn't have to make love with Nash to know that he was a superb lover, a man who would fulfil her most extravagant longings. A man who could re-kindle those bright dreams she had long thought dead in her.

Marrying Nash—the thought would never cease to send a quiver of nerves rushing through her stomach. It sounded so impossible that, crazily, she would almost rather he had proposed a simple affair.

The thought struck her, making her smile wryly, sadly. Being Nash's mistress would be a whole lot easier than being his wife.

The moral Chris Yardley, her boss's mistress? Perish the thought!

'What are you smiling at?' he growled.

'The way you're changing me,' she confessed, trying to restore some order to her once-immaculate self. 'The same way you changed the *Herald*. Do you always start out by reducing everything to chaos?'

'Always,' he grinned, the smile illuminating his face dazzlingly enough to make her pause, staring at him.

'Six months ago,' she told him, 'if you'd told me this was ever going to happen, I'd have laughed my head off.'

'The moment I saw you,' he said, taking her in his arms, 'I knew this was going to happen.' A kiss that made her melt all over again, and then one of those terrifying frowns. 'I trust you're going to inform Duncan Anderson?'

'Oh, Duncan Anderson,' she exclaimed, indignant that he should bring up such a ridiculous topic at a time like this. 'What *have* you got against the poor man?'

'Everything. And he's not a "poor man". He's got plenty.'

'Well, he hasn't got me.' She stroked his face gently. 'And in any case, he won't be around to infuriate you much longer. He phoned me at work yesterday to say he was leaving for America at the weekend.'

'Thank God!' Nash said with heartfelt satisfaction.

'I thought you'd be pleased,' Chris smiled. 'Although he did make me a tempting offer...'

'Indeed?' Nash's face eased into the formidable expression she guessed he reserved for boardroom battles. 'What offer?'

'Oh, he wanted to put me in the movies. He said I had star potential, and I could go a long way. Something about my eyes and hair, and... Oh, I can't remember it all.' Actually, Duncan's offer had been a lot more graphic than that, but by the smouldering expression in Nash's black eyes, it would be unwise to tease him any further. She laughed softly. 'You're right—thank God he's going! When you get that expression on your face, I feel like looking for a hole to climb into. For such a brilliant man, Nash, you can be very blind. Did you really think I was attracted to Duncan? That vain, selfish, immoral little man!'

For answer, his hands slid down to her hips, pulled her against him so that she could feel the thrust of his desire against her, making her close her eyes in dizzy weakness. 'You mean you were stringing me along? All the time?'

'There was never anything between me and Duncan. Oh, yes, he's made more than one pass at me, but I'm not remotely interested. Not in *him*,' she concluded with a smile.

'Minx!' he said threateningly. 'You've made my life a misery for weeks!'

'*You* jumped to the conclusions,' she reminded him innocently. 'Now that you know, will you print my interview with him? It really is rather good...'

'I couldn't refuse if you wanted my heart on a platter,' he sighed, shaking his head ruefully. 'But you ought to be ashamed of yourself, Yardley.'

'Why?' she smiled tenderly. 'I behaved with perfect propriety throughout.'

'Did you, now?' he growled.

'I did. And I intend to do so now. I'm going home.'

'Sure you won't stay the night?' he asked, voice as huskily seductive as Lucifer's.

'Please—you promised!'

'So I did,' he said regretfully. 'I'm going to Manchester again tomorrow, Chris. I wanted to see you so much, and finish off what we started tonight... However, I give you full permission to go the rest of the way—in your dreams tonight.'

'Devil,' she whispered, clinging to him as they walked to the door.

'Am I?' he asked, darkly innocent. 'Maybe that's why I've fallen for an angel like you.'

'You don't know,' she warned. 'I might make you miserable for life!'

'The only way you could ruin my life,' he said softly, 'would be not to marry me. I don't want to do without you any more.'

She clung to him, emotion welling up in her heart. This feeling inside—was it despair or bliss?

*     *     *

As if to prevent Chris from even thinking about her problems, after a very fraught Sunday, Monday morning brought one of those avalanches of work that occasionally made her life scarcely worth living.

Jean was off work with 'flu, and there was no one else she really trusted to be her copy-taster—to organise all the material that came flooding in, and sift out the important stuff for her desk. She was forced to do it herself, with a junior reporter to help, and that morning more copy seemed to have come in than during the whole of the past week.

On top of that, there was the *Honestly...* column. This had been the old *Herald*'s gossip column, written by Chris and Louise Purvis between them. It had been a popular feature. Nash had moved it to the Wednesday Review, and had ordered it to be expanded to take in social and gossip stories on a wider scale. But Louise, one of the *Herald*'s stringers, was currently on her honeymoon in Spain, leaving Chris to cope with the *Honestly...* column alone.

She moved through the mountain of work in top gear, one part of her mind still occupied with the massive and complex subject of Nash. She had spent Sunday at a girlfriend's house, then at Dorothy's, then at another friend's. She had said nothing about Nash to any of them, but her mind had been heavy with fears, doubts, and wild hopes. She had once hated Nash. Yet in time, she had come to understand him, understand and respect him more than she'd ever imagined possible. And now, to desire him physically. But love?

Playing with Doris Holmes's two little boys at her apartment, she had wondered about family life. Was marrying Nash what she'd been born to do? Or would it be an unmitigated disaster, ending in the divorce he'd sworn would never happen? She felt so unsure, so frightened...

She was worn out by the time she made her way to Nash's office just before lunch.

'You all right?' Nash demanded as she dropped the files on his desk.

'Exhausted,' she sighed, and slumped into the padded chair he waved her to. 'And it's freezing outside! I feel like death warmed over.'

His habitual frown eased. 'Poor kid.'

'Fat lot you care,' she accused, trying to rouse her old hostility to him. But she couldn't, and to her horror, the remark came out almost tender mockery.

'I do care,' he said matter-of-factly. 'I'll treat you to dinner tonight. How's that?'

She arched her back to rub her aching neck. Nash's glittering eyes dropped to the thrust of her breasts against the deep-red dress, then up to her face again. It was like a game—I want you, you want me, but we both have to wait...

'Sore neck?' he enquired silkily.

'Just nerves.'

'Ah. Nerves.' He rose, lithe as a panther, and came round the back of her chair, sure fingers massaging the tense tops of her shoulders, the ache in the back of her neck.

'Oh, that's good,' she moaned, closing her eyes as his strong hands expertly eased the tension away. She knew it was never wise to let him touch her, but it was so delicious...

'Have you been thinking about what I said to you on Saturday night?' he asked, his deep voice rough, as though touching her had the same effect on him as it had on her.

'All the time,' she admitted dreamily.

'And?'

Nervously, jokily, she said, 'Perhaps I'll go and become a nun.'

Steel fingers bit into her flesh for a moment, making her gasp. 'I trust that's a bad joke,' he said softly.

'I don't know what it is.' The delicate muscles were knotting up again, she could feel them tense under his fingers. 'I hardly know where I am any more.'

'You're right here with me.' He swung her round to face him, and jolted her with piercingly dark eyes. 'Where you're going to stay, my sweet.'

'But *marriage*,' she said, twisting her fingers restlessly. 'It seems so impossible, Nash. We've been fighting each other for such a long time——'

'Oh, come on.' He cut through her sentence with a touch of his old impatience. 'Are you trying to deny the way you feel about me?'

'No.' She couldn't lie, not under that gaze. 'But people who are attracted to each don't necessarily get married,' she said in a small voice.

'Oh?' Nash's passionate, commanding mouth slanted into an ironic line. 'What else do they do?'

'They——' For the life of her, she couldn't stop the blood from rushing to her face. 'They get to know each other better,' she stammered clumsily.

'Are you proposing an affair?' he enquired, the corners of his mouth twitching as though he weren't sure whether to laugh or frown.

She looked at him, studying the dark face that was almost never out of her thoughts or her dreams these days. She'd once thought him ugly. Crazy. He was magnificent, with that devastating mouth, the laughter-lines that softened the harshness of those black, direct eyes. A face to fantasise about, to melt your bones.

'Something like that,' she said, the phrase intended to sound light, but coming out husky.

'You never cease to amaze me!' He leaned down to do what she'd been aching for him to do all day—kiss her.

At that moment, the office door swung open to admit Anita Klaus. The narrow brown eyes widened in astonishment, then darkened to stormy anger as she saw Nash about to kiss Chris's trembling mouth.

The sight of Anita sent a cold shock rippling through her system, and Chris jumped up, blushing furiously. 'I was just leaving,' she said shortly. 'I've got a lot of work on my plate.' She fled, oblivious to anything but her need to get away.

Back in her office, she found that her hands were shaking. Nash had only to come near her to make her dissolve. Damn Anita! She really felt she hated her now. Get a grip on yourself, girl, she told herself fiercely. Deep breaths, calm thoughts.

Someone opening the door interrupted her thoughts, and she turned on her swivel chair. It was Anita, and Chris's body tensed as if to brace itself against an attack. But when Anita spoke, her voice was quiet.

'I want to talk to you, Chris.'

'All right,' Chris said with an effort, and pointed to one of the chairs.

'It's about Nash. And you. And me.' Anita's eyes met Chris's, but there was no anger in them now. 'Let's start with me,' she said. 'I don't think you've ever liked me. But then, you haven't understood me. I'm an ambitious woman, Chris. Not ambitious in the way you are. You want to be a good journalist, a good person, and I guess, a good wife and mother. Am I right?'

'I suppose so,' Chris nodded, taken aback.

'My ambitions are for money and power.' Anita smiled rather drily. She had had her mane of hair permed yesterday, and she was looking sophisticated and sleek in a dark suit with a red silk bow. 'This is supposed to be a liberated age, but having ambitions like mine is still very unfeminine. It makes you unpopular.' She shrugged elegant shoulders. 'However, that's my problem, not yours. Let's move on to Nash. When he bought out the *Herald*, I could see that here was a man who was really going places. I knew that my real chance had come. Not to marry him, as you all thought, but to impress him enough for him to take me with him on his way up. Can you understand the difference?'

'Yes,' Chris said warily, still unready to trust Anita, or anything she said.

'Good.' The dark eyes gleamed with what might have been triumph. 'Because I've started realising my own ambitions.'

'Through Nash?'

'Yes. He's appointed me advertising manager for both the *Herald* and the Manchester *Sunday News*.'

'Oh,' Chris leaned back, grey eyes thoughtful. 'Congratulations, Anita. That's a big step up.'

'It is. And when Nash buys his next paper, I've got a chance of moving up still further.' She met Chris's eyes. 'I'm good at my job, Chris. Working for Nash Canfield is the biggest break I'll ever get, it's my chance to shine. I want to keep on working for him. And that brings me to you.'

'Go on.'

'You and I have had our differences. But it's time to bury them.'

'Just like that?' Chris said with a little smile.

'The last thing I want is to be on bad terms with my boss's wife.'

Chris's smile faded. 'What makes you think I'm going to marry Nash?'

Anita laughed, showing pearly teeth. 'Oh, you will. Unless you're mad. He adores you, and you adore him. I know.' She shook her head. 'And no, I've never been Nash's lover. I've tried to give that impression and I've even——' She shrugged. 'Well, I'm not scrupulous about the means I use to get ahead. But Nash never wanted me, not like that. I think he's been in love with you right from the start. A couple of weeks ago, he came round to my place one night, in a fury with you. He didn't tell me what it was all about, but I knew then just how much he cared for you. I gave him a glass of wine, and we talked—about you, your father, and the future for all of us. That was when he first told me he might be buying the *Sunday News*, and when he suggested that I might be appointed advertising manager for both papers.' She laid her fingers across her breast. 'Hand on heart, Chris, that's all that happened. I was an absolute bitch to you the next day, and I know I probably gave you a couple of weeks of misery.'

Chris could only stare at her. Then nothing had happened that night...and Nash would never have known about the cruel game Anita had been playing behind his back all this time!

'I was hateful,' Anita said quietly, reading Chris's thoughts. 'But at the time I was bursting with triumph and excitement—and spite.'

Chris found her voice. 'Spite?'

'I came from a poor family,' Anita said gently. 'Like Nash. I've had to work for all the goodies in my life. Can you imagine how I felt about you? You had everything—beauty, brains, education. You had a powerful father, you were the darling of everyone at the *Herald*——'She broke off with a little laugh. 'My feelings for you were always coloured with envy, Chris. That's why I was always rather a cow to you. Maybe I hurt you, but I've been hurt much more in my own life, remember that. More than you'll ever know.' Anita stood up. 'You were born an angel, Chris. I was born a bitch. But your man doesn't want me, and I don't want him. I'd like to call a truce from now on.'

'I'm perfectly willing to go along with a truce,' Chris said with a rather wry expression. 'But I wouldn't count on my being Mrs Nash Canfield.'

'You couldn't live without him,' Anita contradicted calmly. 'Nash has been in your blood ever since the day he took over the *Herald*. It's been in your face for months, as plain as daylight.'

'Never!' Chris said indignantly. 'I've never disliked a man so much at first sight in my life!'

Anita smiled. 'I could see your hands shaking when you spoke to him. I've known you for a long time, remember. There's not a great deal you can hide from me. He's the right man for you. Nash Canfield is going to go a long, long way in life, Chris. And you'll go with him. He's due for his K in a year or so; have you thought of that?'

'His K?'

'A knighthood. Sir Nash Canfield. Which, if you plight your troth, will make you Lady Canfield. That has a nice ring to it, doesn't it?'

Without waiting for an answer, Anita walked out of the office, closing the door behind her.

Chris found herself looking up at the painting opposite her. It was a beautiful thing, really, dazzlingly beautiful. How she'd hated it at first! It had taken her weeks to see what a magnificent work of art it really was.

Poor Anita. For the first time, she was feeling compassion for the thrusting, aggressive advertising manager. It was amazing how kindly you could feel towards someone, once you'd stopped suspecting them of sleeping with the man you loved!

And she believed Anita. It was inconceivable, given Nash's feelings towards her, that he would have been Anita's lover. Yet she still felt as though a heavy weight had been lifted from her mind. It had been darkening her thoughts for a long time, coming between her and Nash. Now she was realising just how Nash must have felt about Duncan.

Like a pair of silly children, they had both been trying to make the other jealous, playing a foolish, dangerous game with their love. But now the game was coming to an end.

And the reality was just beginning.

# CHAPTER NINE

'BRILLIANT.' Nash studied the Wednesday Review page in the foyer of the *Herald* building. He glanced up at Chris with bright black eyes. 'I'd say you've come of age, as a journalist.'

'I'd say it's having a brilliant editor,' Chris smiled. 'Though I never thought I'd say that.'

'Oh, you're good enough at your job,' Nash nodded, folding the paper, and opening the door for her. 'Too good, maybe.'

'How—too good?'

'You pour everything into your work. All the emotion that should have been going into a family life. And a romance.'

'Oh, you're so clever,' she retorted, knowing her sharp reaction stemmed from the fact that what Nash had said had struck home with hurtful accuracy. 'I hate being psychoanalysed!'

'I'm not trying to psychoanalyse,' he replied, unruffled. 'It doesn't matter from now on, in any case. You're going to have your own family to fulfil your life.'

'Always assuming I do marry you,' she reminded him, 'and even then, assuming that I decide to have any children so early in my marriage.'

'Our marriage.' The quiet words held a calm authority which silenced her for a moment. 'Care to eat out, or should I just whip something up at the apartment?'

'I'll risk your cooking,' she decided. She clung to his muscular arm as they hurried through the whirling snow to Nash's car. The bitter cold had brought pink to her fresh complexion, and Nash's eyes were appreciative as he kissed her mouth hard in the car.

'Damned thing about your being an employee,' he muttered, inhaling the sweet smell of her hair, 'is I can't kiss you at work.'

'Which is just as well.' She rubbed her cool cheeks against his hand like a cat. 'Or I wouldn't get a word written.'

It was some time before he pulled out and started the drive across town to his apartment. 'Tell me something,' he invited, lights from oncoming cars flitting across his rugged face. 'If you did to decide to marry me, what would your reasons be?'

'What a question!' she said, laughing. Nash didn't answer her smile, though, and she shook her hair back, thinking. 'Well, why do people normally get married?'

'You tell me.'

'For security, I suppose. I mean,' she said with a hint of irony, 'being married to you would make my life very much more comfortable, wouldn't it?'

'Is that meant to be a joke?' he growled, eyes glittering at her ominously.

'A very bad one,' she said in a small voice. She was always making the mistake of imagining Nash didn't have any feelings, that his hard-as-bronze exterior went right through to the core. And then she went and said something idiotic, and realised she'd angered and hurt him. 'The truth is that people get married for love,' she said in the same miserable voice. 'And deep down, that's why I always imagined I'd get married. But——'

'But?'

'I don't know if—if you really love me, Nash.' The admission was oddly painful, even humiliating. As though she were begging him to tell her he cared. Her next words were in a whisper. 'Do you?'

'I've asked you to marry me, haven't I?'

It was no answer, and left her feeling worse than before. 'There's the other side, too,' she went on. 'Whether I really care enough for you to go through with it all.'

He was silent for a few seconds. 'Let's go home and talk about that, hmm?'

It was cold enough to warrant Nash lighting a log-fire in the marble fireplace. She curled up in front of the rising flames with the brandy he gave her, feeling the deep mood of happiness come over her while he cooked. Life was so easy when she simply gave in to what Nash wanted. She looked into the crimson glow of the fire. As always, he had taken complete control of her. Yet now there was no resentment in her. Was she, God forbid, learning to like being dominated by Nash Canfield?

He rustled up a herb omelette with bacon and mush-rooms, and they ate in intimate contentment, discussing the day's work lazily while they relaxed.

Afterwards, she put the dishes into the dishwasher, and came through to find him sitting in front of the fire. He held out his arms to her silently, and she nestled into them, like a bird finding haven in the strong branches of an oak.

The moment seemed to go on for ever, as he held her in his arms, his cheek resting against the silken sheen of her hair. Her fingers stirred gently against his shoulder, absently tracing the hard pattern of his muscles; they lay in the sensual warmth of the fire, listening to its soft, contented cracklings and whisperings. The only other

sound to disturb the deep stillness was the patter of the
rain, now soft, now loud, against the windows.

'You mean the world to me,' he said quietly. 'Shall
we get married next month?'

The words seemed to pierce her, sending a kind of
pleasure-pain right through her heart. Yet some per-
verse devil of doubt made her question him, as though
pleading again for that reassurance.

'That's so soon...'

Her punishment came with fingers that knotted in her
hair to pull her roughly close to him. 'Either you're very
blind,' he rumbled, 'or you're playing some kind of
game, Chris. Which is it?'

'Don't,' she begged, frightened of his intensity.

'You drive me crazy,' he said in a rough whisper, and
kissed the corners of her mouth gently, then the
throbbing pulse at her throat. 'Sometimes I could——'

Chris moaned quietly, the touch of his lips almost a
pain against her soft skin. Every nerve in her body felt
as though it wanted to jump out of her skin as he un-
fastened her blouse and bent to kiss the full swell of her
breasts. He whispered her name roughly, his breath warm
against the petal-soft skin.

The old, sweet magic was rushing through her blood
at his touch, her pulses racing like a drummer gone mad,
her breath coming shallow, her mouth suddenly dry...
She ran her fingers restlessly through his hair as he
pressed his dark face against the satin skin of her breasts,
drawing in the sweet smell of her skin. Dear God, if this
wasn't love, then what was? It was a consuming hunger
that left no room for a single other emotion in her whole
being.

Only the need for him, the need to give herself to him,
mattered. She cried out loud as Nash's mouth found the

rose-tipped peaks, became fierce with passion, sucking her into a dizzy vortex of pleasure. There was the same pleasure-pain in touching him, running her palms hungrily over his muscled body, beneath his silk shirt.

'My sweet Chris,' he said huskily, pulling the garment off impatiently. He had an athlete's body, lithe-waisted and deep-chested, hard with muscle. A man's body, deeply exciting in a way that it was impossible not to respond to, the tanned skin hot and smooth to her touch.

She was trembling as he came to her again, the light from the flames flickering on his smooth skin.

'I've been aching for this,' he said, his voice ragged in his throat. 'You're in my blood, Christine, like a fever. I've wanted you ever since I first set eyes on you, my love...'

She was murmuring his name helplessly as he knelt in front of her and took her face tenderly in his hands, bending to kiss her. She couldn't have resisted him even if she'd wanted to, now. All rebellion was gone, her will dazed by him. Her lips surrendered to his desire, opening to him helplessly as he caressed her neck, her shoulders, cupping her full breasts in his hands.

His naked skin was warm and smooth against hers as his lips brushed her swollen nipples. Touching him was a voyage of discovery, an entry into a new world. All her life seemed to have been moving towards this point, this meeting with him, here and now. Her fingertips were timid, feather-light as they traced the lines of his back, his chest, the taut curve of his ribcage, his hard, flat stomach. She wanted him so badly, wanted to know about him; but she was so afraid, so shy. Until Nash drew her hand gently down, making her trace the pattern of his desire with trembling fingers.

'Nash,' she whispered shakily. The depth of her own reactions was frightening her. His body was thrustingly, intensely male, eager for her. As she grew bolder he gasped, deep in his throat, his eyes closing involuntarily as he called her name. 'Chris, my love...'

No kiss could ever be enough now. As though there were ever greater depths to be explored together, their bodies moved together with a restless urgency that was taking its own rhythm. The surge of life in her own body was rising to a flood, taking command of her.

Only when her fuddled mind realised that he was about to make love to her, that this exquisite arabesque of their bodies wasn't just a flirtation, but a preparation for love, did her dazed brain start to function.

'Not yet,' she choked, twisting away from him. 'Not until we're married——'

'Then you *will* marry me!' His dark eyes were bright with triumph as he grinned down at her.

'I didn't say that!'

'That's the only reason that might conceivably stop me now,' he vowed, his mouth roaming hungrily over her face, caressing her eyelids, her temples, the vulnerable line of her exposed throat. 'How I love to see your crystal-goddess image splinter into fragments when I touch you!'

'Oh, Nash,' she said unevenly, 'why on earth do you want to marry *me*? Wouldn't some ravishing society princess suit you a million times better?'

'The answer to that question,' he smiled, 'ought to lie in your own heart, my love. If you don't know how I feel about you by now, I must be doing something wrong.'

She knew how he felt, all right; it was her own feelings that presented the problem! 'But I still feel I don't know you,' she said, almost pleadingly, her hands restlessly caressing his shoulders.

'And when have you ever tried to know me, Christine?' The mockery in the dark eyes covered something else, hurt maybe. 'You've been running away too fast to notice anything.' He drew back, expression wry. 'Just what is it you're running away from, Chris?'

'Myself,' she admitted in an agonising moment of self-knowledge.

'And exactly how far do you imagine you'll get? How long are you going to keep me waiting?'

She didn't have an answer for him. There was only this aching, unrequited need for him inside her, an ache that was too much to bear any longer. If this was love, then she couldn't fight it. She'd never needed any man like this, would never feel like this in her life again. She drew him close to her, offering him her mouth as if begging him to shut out all the questions she couldn't answer.

'Chris,' he said harshly, 'I need you, *now*.'

'Yes,' she pleaded in a shaky whisper. 'Love me, Nash. Love me...'

She awoke hours later, still cradled in his arms. Nash was sleeping quietly, his breathing deep and even. Her head was pillowed on his broad chest, and she could hear his heart beating deep within him, strong and regular.

He must have awoken at some stage, because the fire was still blazing brightly, and a whisper-soft rug had been wrapped around their naked bodies.

Her mind and body still held the memory of Nash's love, warm and bruised and utterly fulfilled. His love-making had been——

There just weren't any words. It was as if she'd built a wall long ago round her heart to keep out joy, and as if Nash had been slowly pulling that wall to pieces, stone by stone, until there was nothing left any more to stop the joy from flooding into her life, filling every corner of her spirit.

She had never known it could be like that. She had known there could be physical pleasure, yes; but not the torrent that had flooded through her, lifting her to heights of ecstasy that had fused her to Nash, body and soul. Making love had been a vitally important step in learning about him—and, more importantly, about herself. Without that knowledge, too deep and mysterious for words, she might never have discovered the truth of her own feelings.

Nash had done more than make love to her. They had become one being, perfect and indivisible. And that was the most wonderful thing that had ever happened to her. It had shown her just how magnificently they were really matched. It had brought her close to Nash in a way that had made all the barriers between them melt away.

The closeness was unbelievable. Mrs Christine Canfield. Suddenly the idea didn't sound ridiculous, or frightening, or impossible any longer. It sounded dazzlingly right, so right that she must have been insane not to have seen it ages ago. Her life had changed forever in the hands of the man she was coming to need more than anything on earth. He'd been so tender with her, so loving. She shivered suddenly, but not with cold, as she remembered their lovemaking. The way Nash had used his hard, flawlessly powerful body to exalt her. His mouth, demanding and commanding, an instrument of pagan delight.

The way she'd clung with helpless passion to his strong shoulders. Giddy and weak, she had felt herself swept off her feet as lightly as a leaf in an autumn gale. And at other times he'd touched her as gently as an angel's wing.

And the things he had said to her. Things erotic enough to make her shudder with passion. Things tender enough to melt the bones inside her...

Right now, there was a lot she wanted to say to him in return.

She sat up, light as a feather, and moved away from Nash without waking him.

The only garment that came to hand was his silk shirt. She picked it up and slipped it on. As she'd anticipated, it came half-way down her thighs, and in this effective covering she padded barefoot to the kitchen to make them coffee. In the mirror beside the percolator, her face looked back at her, flushed, bright-eyed and soft-lipped, more beautiful than any cosmetics could have made it. 'For God's sake,' she muttered at her reflection, 'must you give the whole game away?'

Yet she would have shouted it from the rooftops if she could. She hadn't felt so alive, so happy, for years. The inner radiance she felt seemed to have flooded her whole spirit, giving her a new kind of beauty, a new kind of joy.

Would the exultation last? Even the challenge posed by that question somehow only added brilliance to the way she felt, giving zest to her love. Life with Nash Canfield was never going to be dull, not ever.

There was suddenly so much to do. A wedding to plan, a whole life to map out with Nash...

She brought the two cups of coffee through to him. An odd feeling, knowing there were always going to be two cups of coffee from now on. Two people, one life.

He was magnificent in sleep, one muscular arm stretched out across the place where she'd lain, his dark face relaxed and open. Adoring him helplessly, she slipped under the blanket and laid her head on his broad shoulder, feeling his strength and warmth envelop her. This wonderful, wonderful man, who'd given her everything...

She only needed to brush his lips with her own to wake him. He smiled at her dreamily, his eyes filled with love.

'I've made coffee,' she murmured.

'Will you still be here if I wake up?' he asked softly.

'I'll always be here,' she smiled, touching his warm lips with her fingertips. 'And I want you awake. I want to tell you the truth.'

'What truth?'

'That I love you, Nash, with all my heart and mind. That I've probably always loved you, but been too blind to see it. That you're the most wonderful thing that has ever happened to me. That my only desire in the world is to make you as happy as I can. For the rest of our lives together.'

Nash stared at her with a strange expression on his face. 'You'll marry me?'

'Tomorrow, if you like.' And she knew that she meant the words, now and for ever. 'Can you forgive me for the way I've treated you? I've been such a fool, always arguing with you, trying to run away from you, making you jealous with Duncan Anderson——'

'Not exactly jealous,' he contradicted. 'Just terrified that you shared his views of love and marriage.' He kissed her parted lips. 'You see, you're so precious to me that when I heard you repeating Duncan Anderson's opinions, I got this horrible fear that you'd never be able to respond to the kind of love I wanted to give you.'

'I was only trying to annoy you,' she confessed in a small voice. 'Trying to get you back. I was so convinced you were having an affair with Anita...'

'Yes, I understand that now. If I'd had any inkling of what Anita was doing to you, I'd have understood a long time ago.' He smiled drily. 'But given that nothing was going on between me and Anita, I could never understand what you were so jealous about!'

'You must have thought I was a complete neurotic. But I really suffered.' Chris twined her arms round his neck, staring up at his face with adoring eyes. 'My God,' she whispered, almost too full to speak. 'If you only knew how much I love you, Nash.'

'I only have to look into my own heart,' he smiled. 'Then I know everything.' His eyes narrowed smokily as his hand touched her cheek, brushing her full mouth, then caressed downwards to her breasts. Chris felt her senses suddenly swim as his fingers trailed over the soft swell of her woman's body, cupping her breast with desirous possession.

'Chris.' His voice was low and husky as he whispered her name. 'If you knew what those words mean to me...'

'I'd have said them ages ago if I hadn't been so arrogant and stupid,' she whispered.

'Then say them again, now,' he commanded, his voice a husky growl.

She did. Then, blindly, she lifted her lips to his, yielding to the mastery of his kiss, shuddering at the sweet invasion he was inflicting on her mouth. His power and passion overwhelmed her, exalted her. This was how it would always be. This ecstasy was only a tiny fragment of the ocean of love that lay in store for them.

'This was meant for much later,' Nash said gently, reaching out for his jacket, where it lay over the arm of the sofa. He took something out of the pocket. 'But I think now is the right moment for it, after all.'

She fumbled the neat leather box open. The diamond, flawless as her happiness, blazed in the firelight. Her hands were shaking helplessly as she lifted it out, and watched it dazzle in her fingertips. 'I've wanted you from the minute I saw you,' he said quietly, looking into her eyes. 'First it was simply desire. You're my ideal of perfection in a woman, Chris. Slender, graceful, with those dazzling eyes and that silky hair——' He smiled, touching her lips. 'But there was much, much more to come. I hardly knew that I was falling in love with you, day by day, hour by hour. There was so much to find out about you, like your gentleness, your intelligence, your spirit. You got into my blood, like a fever. I've always dreamed of a woman who could stand beside me. Work beside me, plan, take decisions with me. And you're that woman, Chris. I want you, all of you, for ever!'

She gave him the ring. 'Put it on,' she pleaded. As he slid the hoop over her finger, their lips met with tenderness, with love. 'I'm not wearing a stitch,' she said quietly. It was true—her earrings were lying on the carpet, and Nash had even pulled the velvet ribbon from her golden hair. 'And I'm glad. Because this ring is the first thing I'll put on in my new life. And the last thing I'll ever take off.'

Ages later, she was lying in his arms, her heart pounding against her ribs, more blissfully happy than she could ever have dreamed. 'Poor Miss Claws,' she said gently. 'And I was so suspicious of her...'

'Never mind Miss Claws, or anyone else,' he commanded. 'It's just you and me, from now on.' His mouth brushed her eyelids. 'You know I can't leave the *Herald* without you with me? I need someone to be at my side, my partner in running not just a single newspaper, but a whole group of newspapers. I'm afraid the Wednesday Review will have to do without you from the day of our wedding on.'

'Yes,' Chris smiled, tracing the line of his face with her fingers. 'I know that. The *Herald* is part of my life now, but only a part. And only because it's yours. Because you are my life, from now until eternity.'

'We'll be together,' he nodded. 'In our work, in our love, always together. We've got so much in common.'

'So much in common... Why was I so stupid?' she wondered. 'And why are you so clever?'

Nash shook his head. 'No, Chris. I'm just very, very lucky. And sometimes I can be very stupid, believe me. It took me months to reconcile myself with the way I felt about you. I knew from the start that you really were the woman I'd been waiting for all my life. But there were so many reasons why I had to keep you at a safe distance, always staying at arm's length.'

'What reasons?'

'The fact that your father had just died, meaning you were emotionally highly vulnerable. The fact that I'd just bought out the paper your family founded.' He grinned. 'And, not least, the fact that you disagreed with just about everything I wanted to do with the *Herald*. I could hardly ask you to marry me while you were sulking and spitting at me the whole time, could I?'

Chris felt her cheeks redden with shame. 'Oh, Nash, I've been so stupid about you. I thought you were destroying the *Herald*, when in reality you were making it live again.'

'There was a certain immaturity,' he admitted wryly, as though he hated to criticise her, even in the slightest way. 'Something which I felt you had to deal with yourself, in your own way. I couldn't bully you out of it. I just had to wait until you saw the light with your own eyes.'

'That took long enough,' she confessed.

'Yes,' he admitted drily. 'It did, rather. But I had enough faith in your character to know that you would settle down eventually, and that, if I forced myself to hold back until you did, it would be far better in the end. But there were times when you did try my patience a little...'

'You certainly frightened me out of my wits sometimes,' she smiled, her eyes soft. 'I'm not saying I didn't deserve it—God knows I did. And I'll probably keep deserving it for a while longer. But you used to terrify me!'

'I know,' he said ruefully. 'But you scared me, too, in a different way. Once I'd accepted that I wanted you, and only you—and that no other woman could ever make me happy—I started getting cold feet. I used to wonder sometimes whether it would ever work out! And that used to drive me crazy. When I was at my grimmest, I was most afraid, most full of doubt.'

'Did you ever doubt that I'd be yours in the end?' she asked.

'Sometimes,' he admitted, 'I wondered whether I'd ever see love in your eyes, and not distrust or hate!'

'What do you see in them now?'

'I see love,' he nodded. 'And I see the knowledge that you have me, in the palm of your little hand. And that's the way I'll always be, Chris. Yours.'

He brushed her lips with his own. She looked up into his midnight-dark eyes, losing herself in their potent depths.

'Don't say any more, just yet,' she pleaded. 'So much has happened just lately that I'm afraid this is just a dream, and that any puff or breeze will blow you away from me.'

'I love you,' he whispered.

'Ahhh...' She shuddered with pleasure. 'That's the first time you've ever said that to me.'

'Is it?' he smiled.

'Yes.' She opened her eyes dreamily. 'And it felt wonderful.'

'I've said it to you so many times—in my mind. If only you knew...'

'I do, now,' she nodded emphatically. 'Say it again. Please?'

'When you've earned it,' he teased. He touched her mouth with his fingertips. 'We're getting married next month, Chris.'

'Is that an order?' she murmured. 'Or do I have any say in the matter?'

'None whatsoever.'

'Ah, well, you already have my soul,' she told him. 'Why not take the rest of me?'

'That's an offer,' he said, sliding down beside her, eyes promising passion that would shake her to the core, 'that I can't refuse. Now...' His lips were already tasting her naked skin, roaming with hungry appreciation across her woman's body. 'What was it you wanted me to say?'

# You'll flip . . . your pages won't!
## Read paperbacks *hands-free* with

# Book Mate • I

**The perfect "mate" for all your romance paperbacks**

**Traveling • Vacationing • At Work • In Bed • Studying • Cooking • Eating**

Perfect size for all standard paperbacks, this wonderful invention makes reading a pure pleasure! Ingenious design holds paperback books OPEN and FLAT so even wind can't ruffle pages – leaves your hands free to do other things. Reinforced, wipe-clean vinyl-covered holder flexes to let you turn pages without undoing the strap . . . supports paperbacks so well, they have the strength of hardcovers!

Pages turn WITHOUT opening the strap.

**SEE-THROUGH STRAP**

Reinforced back stays flat.

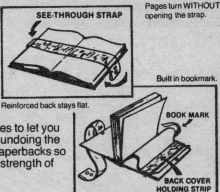

Built in bookmark.

BOOK MARK

BACK COVER HOLDING STRIP

10˝ x 7¼˝, opened.
Snaps closed for easy carrying, too.

# Harlequin American Romance

---

## Romances that go one step farther...
## American Romance

Realistic stories involving people you can relate to and care about.

Compelling relationships between the mature men and women of today's world.

Romances that capture the core of genuine emotions between a man and a woman.

Join us each month for four new titles wherever paperback books are sold.
Enter the world of American Romance.

---